SAFARI

Casablanca! Crossroads of international espionage . . . a glittering, decadent city minutes away from Africa's dark heart, where jungle drums still beat their deadly insistent rhythms.

Casablanca! Where America's Number 1 counter-intelligence agent was to face his most explosive assignment.

SAFARI FOR SPIES

Nick Carter

A STAR BOOK
published by
the Paperback Division of
W. H. ALLEN & Co. Plc

A Star Book
Published in 1979
by the Paperback Division of
W. H. Allen & Co. Plc
44 Hill Street, London W1X 8LB

Reprinted 1981
Reprinted 1987

First published in Great Britain by
Universal-Tandem Publishing Co. Ltd, 1969
Reprinted 1970, 1975

Printed and bound in Great Britain by
Anchor Brendon Ltd, Tiptree, Essex

ISBN 0 352 30584 3

Dedicated to
The Men of the Secret Services
of the
United States of America

YOU ARE ACCUSED

THERE was not, so far as he knew, the slightest reason for anyone outside his official reception committee to be waiting for him in Dakar, but somebody else most certainly was. And it was much too early in the game for that.

Nicholas J. Huntington Carter stepped off the jet into the cool African morning feeling both overdressed and oddly naked. New Panama hat, slim briefcase practically covered with initials, bone-handled walking cane to match the stiffness of his back . . . all this, when all he really felt like wearing was a set of bust khakis and a knotted handkerchief. But what the hell. This was a job, not a picnic. And it was going to be a sticky one, for all the diplomatic camouflage.

Something about using his own name made him feel stripped to the buff yet painted over with signs blazoning out his identity and purpose. HI, SPY! the invisible label announced. THE NAME IS CARTER. NICK CARTER. SECRET AGENT N-3, KILLMASTER FOR AXE. Beneath, in smaller print, the imaginary sign confided the inscription across his chest: TROUBLESHOOTER WITH LICENCE TO KILL. He could almost read the tempting invitation offering him as a target to anyone on the opposite side of the espionage fence. COME AND GET ME, RED, said the bullseye over his heart. READY, AIM, FIRE!

But nobody did. At least not right now.

It was probably because he felt so exposed that Nick sensed the eyes upon him from the moment he stepped into the airport building. They were watching him from behind a newspaper while Tad Fergus of the Embassy whisked him through the brief formalities of passage through Senegal and into the main arrival centre to meet Liz Ashton and the two officials from Nyanga. And they stayed with him until they saw whom he had met.

Raphael Sendhor and Oscar Adebe, Foreign Minister

and Vice-President respectively, greeted Special U.S. Ambassador Carter with cool courtesy.

"We welcome you," their liquid accents said while their calm expressions denied, "on behalf of President Makombe, our country and ourselves. You wish perhaps for refreshment and rest before we complete our journey?"

"Thank you, gentlemen, but no," said Nick, his voice as soft as theirs and his manner as restrained. "I'd like to get to Abimako as soon as possible."

They nodded, satisfied, two very young and strikingly handsome ebony men from the six-month-old Republic of Nyanga.

"You will permit me, then," said Sendhor, bowing slightly. "The President's plane awaits. I shall lead the way. Your luggage . . . ?"

"I have taken the liberty," said Tad. "It is on the plane."

Two multicoloured flowing robes rustled and glided ahead across the marbled floor. Nick followed, flanked by Liz and Tad. The back of his neck was crawling, and the feeling had nothing to do with the gangling, red-headed Tad or the darkly attractive Liz Ashton. The sensation he got from looking at her was much more pleasant than the warning tingle that kept his instincts tuned in to some alien presence. Not just something unfamiliar; something wrong.

He saw the eyes upon him, bulbous and frog-lidded staring over the top of a French newspaper. They rolled over him like greased ball bearings, and with such intensity that he could literally feel them on his body. They were ugly, glass-pale eyes, and the oddly green cast of the skin rendered them even more horribly colourless.

Nick nodded attentively at something Tad was saying and scrutinized the watcher as they approached. He'll know me anywhere, Nick thought And I'll know him.

"Do you recognize the fellow watching us from behind the newspaper?" he said conversationally. "Left front. He's very interested. Miss Ashton, how do you like living in Abimako?"

"Why, I—I like it very much," she stammered, slightly

off-balance. "What man?"

The newspaper went up like a flag as they passed.

"Good God," murmured Fergus. "Literally green in the face. Jealous of the company we keep? Never saw him before. I'd remember if I had."

Nick grunted softly to himself. The three Americans followed the young African leaders out of the terminal and back on to the airfield where President Julian Makombe's private plane waited.

The pale pink glow of early morning turned into the orange blaze of a hot day as they stepped into the plane.

Moments later the two-engined Skycraft was soaring high above the gleaming coastline of West Africa towards the tiny capital of newly independent and deeply troubled Nyanga.

Nick put aside his cane and stretched his long legs beneath the seat in front of him. Sendhor and Adebe had finished lavishing cool courtesies upon him and were sitting together in silence. Tad Fergus and Liz Ashton, respectively First and Second Secretaries of the bombed American Embassy in Nyanga, were sunk in a silence of their own, wondering just what this sleek-haired, bespectacled and almost too-handsome man with the rakish chin and foppish cane could possibly do about the mess in Nyanga.

Nice looking, thought Liz. Probably conceited. Special emissary. Big deal. What does he know about Africa and its problems? Suppose he thinks this is going to be another Washington cocktail party and a lot of backroom baloney. He'll learn. Sure he'll learn, she thought resentfully. And go back home to report the facts while the whole damn country blows itself to bits.

Tad Fergus chewed his lips thoughtfully. Nyanga was his second assignment in Africa, and he wanted it to last. He loved the country, its golden beaches and white deserts, its stretches of hilly scrubland that changed from pearl-pink to blazing red to deep purple with the passing of each day, its proud handsome people who wanted so very much to be the masters of their own destiny, the flamingoes and the bark canoes on its cool, dangerous waters, and the sharp bite of air untainted by the belch of factory fumes. Even the modern capital city of Abimako was clean and airy. Its builders had planned it as a tree-lined, streamlined model city of the new Africa. But something was going horribly wrong. He glanced sideways at Nick Carter. So. This was the man who was supposed to set everything right. Funny that he'd never heard of him before.

The small plush presidential plane droned smoothly on. Nick stared out of the window at the vividly tinted clouds and wondered if a killer spy was really the right man for a delicately diplomatic mission. But wholesale murder was never delicate, and diplomacy had already fallen on its face.

He looked down as Sendhor called his name and pointed. The plane banked sharply and circled low over drifting wisps of smoke. What lay beneath the smoke was the remnant of a ravaged village. Charred stumps of huts pointed starkly at the sky, and what was once a grain field was a vast black scar. There was not a living soul or an animal in sight.

"Yesterday," Tad said tightly, his red head thrusting past Nick's. "In broad daylight, with a band of kids in front of them. No one believed they really would attack. But they did. A few of the women in the fields got away. A handful of men and children wound up in the hospital. The rest—just didn't leave. The troops got here last night. Too late, as you can see. The bush telegraph isn't quite as miraculous as people like to think." His last comment was full of bitterness, as though outsiders like this Carter were full of misconceptions about the Africa Tad Fergus loved so well.

Nick pulled his eyes away from the scene below. Sendhor and Adebe were looking at him with ill-concealed dislike. Tad's face was an angry mask and tears trembled in the corners of Liz's eyes.

"They think *we* could do a thing like that," she whispered.

"Who else?" said Sendhor, his fine lips twisted with contempt.

"We'll find out who else," Nick answered flatly, his eyes flint-hard and his jaw set. "Let's get this plane to Abimako and get on with it."

Theoretically, he knew "who else." The problem was to find him. And deal with him accordingly.

Nick's role as a high ranking diplomat on a special trouble-shooting mission had begun with an urgent summons followed by detailed instructions from Hawk, who seemed to think that one free weekend between assignments was enough vacation for any man. Carter had mumbled to himself, said goodbye to the girl and hopped the first plane home to New York for briefing and new orders. The head of AXE had long since given up the luxury of spare time for himself and was apparently under the impression that his top secret operative would, too.

When Nick had gone to meet the others in a small conference room at United Nations headquarters he had already transformed himself into a top State Department official with the mental intensity of a Robert Kennedy, the cool geniality and drive of a Sargent Shriver, and the quietly determined bearing of the Secretary of Defence. He hoped he had chosen suitable models.

The Secretary of State for African Affairs sucked quietly on his pipe and waited for Polikov to finish with his small talk and settle down. His eyes wandered over the group around the table and he thought suddenly how insignificant the meeting seemed and yet how important it really was. Four men and himself versus the disintegration of a newborn African nation *and* a probable showdown with the U.S.S.R. There were other channels of mediation, true, but he knew instinctively that in spite of all the talk that might follow failure, the AXE mission was their only real chance to save a situation that had grown rapidly from minor incident to murderous chaos and from slight mistrust to hatred and suspicion.

Polikov and Mbanzi, of course, had never heard of AXE. The Secretary for African Affairs devoutly hoped they never would. Sending a spy with the title of Killmaster on a fact-finding expedition was scarcely a move calculated to inspire confidence in the plaintiff. In fact, it could just blow everything to hell. But the President himself, with the full support of the National Security Council, had felt that this was a job for Hawk's department. He had mentioned Nick Carter specifically by name.

The Secretary tapped his pipe on the huge ashtray and cleared his throat.

"Gentlemen," he began. "As you all know, I have already held a preliminary meeting with the representative from Nyanga, which I followed with discussions on a presidential level. The Russian Ambassador in Washington has filed a protest with the United States. As a result we are meeting here today in a effort to clarify the situation and agree upon our course of action."

He shifted uncomfortably in his chair, thoroughly disliking the formal language he felt obliged to use. Hawk eyed him sympathetically and chomped quietly on his evil-smelling cigar.

"We have all met informally," "Dusty" Thompson continued. "Now I should like to explain why each of us is here." Serge Polikov produced a knowing smile. Nick disliked him instantly. "Dr. Tom Mbanzi is the head of the United Nations delegation from Nyanga, which became an independent nation on September 7th of last year. He is here because President Makombe of his country prefers to conduct negotiations under the auspices of the United Nations, rather than lodge formal governmental protests. If our present efforts fail—and it is vitally important that they do not—both Nyanga and Soviet Russia will call for a meeting of the Security Council, and Nyanga will break off relations with the United States. The Soviet Union," he added, turning a cool gaze upon Polikov, "has mentioned the possibility of employing more drastic measures. I prefer not to detail them at this point." Polikov grinned wolfishly. "Mr. Polikov of the Russian delegation is here at the request of President Makombe as well as of his own government, since their interests in this matter are so closely related. Mr. Hawk and Mr. Carter are here as special representatives of the United States Department of State. The President of Nyanga and the President of the United States have agreed to send a fact-finding mission to Nyanga, one that will be in constant personal contact with both governments. Mr. Hawk is to remain in New York as the liaison official. Mr. Carter will go to Nyanga as trouble-shooter on the scene." Polikov snickered and repeated, "Trouble-shooter!" Thompson regretted his choice of word even as it came out. Polikov would pick it up and make something of it. But Mbanzi was eyeing the Russian with the faintest of frowns. Good. Dusty Thompson had liked this young African scholar and diplomat from the moment of first meeting. And he had not liked the sneering Polikov. Because he was a Russian? Thompson pushed the thought away.

"And now, Dr. Mbanzi, if you would be so good as to describe the situation in your own words?" Thompson gratefully clamped his pipe between his teeth.

Mbanzi began to speak in the lilting, melodic tones of the African who is fluent in many languages and yet still loved his own for its richness and its subtleties. He looked at Hawk and Carter while he spoke, and saw a soldierly old man with gimlet eyes and a youngish athlete with the brow of a savant. Both looked hard as nails and immensely capable.

"I will touch only upon the salient points," Mbanzi said. "Every incident has been documented. I have here more reports for you to read." He laid his hand briefly on a pile of papers. "In substance, my country has been plagued since the day after independence. There has been fighting in the streets of Abimako. Government officials have received mysterious threats. Every day there is shotgun fire. A bomb was exploded in the President's own garden. The Russian Embassy has been bombed. Russian individuals—technicians and government personnel—have been terrorized. Armed bands have started to roam the countryside, threatening to kill and burn and pillage until the people overthrow the government. Everything that could possibly happen to give my country a bad name and to topple its elected officials *is* happening. Even to stirring up peaceful tribespeople and making a rebel army out of them. Hospitals stoned. Missions burned. Our friends from the Soviet Union, murdered." He stared at Dusty, his strong young face accusing. "Why this pattern of terror, when all was peace before? Julian Makombe was elected by the people. They used to honour him. It is not by themselves that they have started to destroy. They have been influenced from outside."

"By what you believe to be undercover agents of the United States," Hawk said bluntly. "Where is your proof, and what could be the motive?"

"The proof is in tape recordings, in photographs, in pamphlets, in the laboratory," Mbanzi said intensely. "An American voice broadcasts incitements to riot. Leaflets are handed out, with drawings and slogans in the American style. Weapons and bomb fragments have been recovered. They are American. As to motive . . ."

Polikov laughed. "It could not be more obvious surely? the whole world knows that the United States Government supported the rightist Karumah for the Presidency and that President Makombe studied in Moscow, that he believes in the Communist dream. It is only too clear why the Americans are trying to make his government fall, to discredit his country and the new regime. And to go so far as to persecute Soviet citizens . . . !"

"I understand that the American Embassy in Nyanga was also bombed," Carter cut in. "You do not regard this as persecution?"

The Russian snorted. "On a weekend, when no one but the domestic staff was there! An obvious cover action. A foolish, naive ploy designed to cloud the issue."

"And these bomb fragments, Dr. Mbanzi," said Nick. Standard American weapons are easy to come by. Voices and pamphlets are simple enough to fake. But bomb fragments do not usually bear the maker's name. May I ask how and where they were analysed?"

"In Moscow," Mbanzi answered, looking at Nick steadily. "By the expert Rubitchev, whose scientific integrity is unassailable."

Polikov smirked.

"We will naturally expect to see the original copy of his report," Hawk said coldly. "The *original*. However. That is a detail we can take up later. First, Dr. Mbanzi, another question. If your government is so convinced that the United States is behind all your present troubles, why did your President specifically request an American investigative mission? Since you have chosen to direct your discussions under the wing of the United Nations, why not request a United Nations team?"

Tom Mbanzi locked gazes with the leathery old man with the pioneer's face and startlingly sharp eyes. At last, he said: "So far, it is a matter between my country and yours. The accused has the right to face the accuser. Even the Russians who have suffered are on our soil and are our responsibility. It is your responsibility, your right, to prove that our accusations are untrue."

It sounded like a declaration of ancient tribal law, or of a law so just and simple that it could only be practised in the new world of the future.

Hawk smiled one of his rare smiles.

"You honour us," he said.

The meeting settled down into a discussion of specifics.

Later, behind the brownstone façade of the AXE branch office near Columbus Circle, Nick went over the final details with Operations and had one last talk with Hawk.

"For almost the first time in my life," he said, "I feel like a fraud. I hate to lie to a man like Tom Mbanzi."

Hawk puffed busily at his cigar. "And for almost the first time in your life, you're going to have to be someone very much like yourself. That's far from being a fraud. And I think you'll find that Julian Makombe won't be too surprised if you're a little unorthodox. He's not expecting a stuffed shirt. Don't try to be one. Mbanzi was sincere when he said what he did about the accuser and the accused. But Makombe went one better. He is *not* convinced that the U.S. is behind his troubles. He's testing us, in a way. But he thinks it's just remotely possible that there may be some other force at work. We *know* there is."

Nick nodded. "It's a familiar pattern. Very much like the operations of CLAW. I sense a fine yellow hand pulling the strings somewhere in the background. With any luck I'll chop it off at the wrist."

"You'll need the luck, because you won't be getting much help. Fergus at the Embassy is a good fellow and may be useful. Then there's our man in Morocco—your orders will tell you how to contact him. But I want you to work through the Embassy as much as possible. On the surface that is."

"'Our man in Morocco,'" Nick grinned faintly. "Sounds very exotic. Was it a movie?" Hawk grunted irritably. "But wouldn't you say Morocco's going to be a little outside my beat?"

Hawk shook his head. "I don't think any place in Africa's going to be outside your beat on this one. An operation of this sort has to be controlled from some relatively big centre. Not from headquarters; that's too far away. It requires a midpoint, large enough for a screen yet accessible to both the target area and the main control centre. Cairo, perhaps. Casablanca, Tangier, or possibly Dakar since it's the closest city of any real size. The trail can lead you anywhere. Don't count on settling down in Abimako. Now, I have a parting gift for you."

Nick raised his eyebrows. "For me? Oh, you shouldn't have!"

Hawk ignored the comment, although a faintly pained look crossed his thin, hard face. He reached beneath his desk and came up with his latest lethal toy: a bone-handled cane.

"Add this to your arsenal," he said.

Nick's room in the Hotel Independence at Abimako was, as Tad had told him when the light plane landed on the smooth new airfield, "nothing gaudy, but quite neat." President Makombe, Sendhor told him, would send a car for him at lunchtime. Nick inspected his new quarters as soon as his entourage had left him. Two large windows looked down on a small square, cool with trees and bright with flowers. The bed was comfortable, the rug thick, the closets ample, and there was a bottle-opener in the compact bathroom. The only drawback was that the room was bugged.

"HE'D BETTER NOT DIE"

It was so obvious it was almost funny. If the system had been any more conspicuous Nick would have been able to sit down at the controls and monitor himself. The telephone fairly bulged with its guilty secret, and the wires that snooped into his room from another were about as discreet as a nude on Broadway.

He left them as they were and sang an incredibly filthy song in a loud, cheerful voice as he unpacked his bags and put his weapons, Wilhelmina, Hugo and Pierre, safely to bed. In case his hearer's English was imperfect he repeated the awful verses first in French and then in Portuguese, finally tossing in a few words of Swahili for special effect. That, he thought with perverse satisfaction, ought to set back American diplomacy a good ten years.

His next move was to call room service and order a hearty breakfast. While waiting for it he showerd briskly and spent fifteen minutes doing a set of Yoga exercises.

Wherever he was, whatever he was doing, Nick found time to spend fifteen minutes each day practising the Yoga exercises that kept his superbly trained, magnificently muscled body at the peak of condition. Because of them, his reflexes were as swift as a striking snake's. He could relax his body even under the duress of extreme pain, and he could hold his breath as long as any man alive. It was largely due to these and related talents that he could go on counting himself among the living. Almost every day of his life offered a challenge to his speed, his skill, his physical strength and amazing flexibility—and his ability to duck.

He lay on the thick carpet clad only in his shorts, willing his muscles into extraordinary positions and thinking idly of the few times he had been obliged to miss his Yoga practice sessions. Once in Palermo, many years before, he had hung in chains for three days without water, food, light or the slightest hope of freeing himself. Finally, a magnificent bluff and a fellow agent had combined to free him. And then there was the time that Van Niekerk had trapped him in the mine-shaft; Nick had had neither the space nor the inclination to go through his entire repertoire, but by contorting his body and controlling his breathing in a certain way, he was able to worm out and surprise the hell out of Van Niekerk.

Nick grinned at the memory and pulled himself to a

cross-legged sitting position. He had done these same exercises on the beach at Tahiti, on a cabin cruiser in the Caribbean, in an Alpine snow shelter, on a desert island, in the bedroom of a countess and in the mansion of an exiled queen. And now, on a carpet in Africa. He drew in his abdomen until it seemed to cling to his backbone. The muscles of his chest and shoulders stood out in relief.

Even though he was giving every ounce of his concentration to the task at hand he sensed there was someone at the door even before he heard the knock. Breakfast, he thought hungrily, and was on his feet pulling on his trousers when the knock came.

"Come in."

He had left the door unlocked for the waiter, But it was not the waiter who came in.

Liz Ashton stood in the doorway staring at the bare expanse of his chest.

"Oh," she said, and blushed as suddenly as if she'd thrown a switch to light up her face. "I'm terribly sorry. I should have called you first."

"Please, no apologies," Nick said cheerfully. "Come in. Turn around for a moment, if you like, while I make myself presentable."

"Oh, it isn't that you're not presentable," she began, and stopped suddenly. Hesitantly, she made her way to a chair and sat down on the edge. But she did not avert her eyes as Nick took a fresh shirt from the bureau drawer. She stared at him and thought he looked so much better without his glasses or his shirt and with his hair half-damp and tousled. But she could scarcely encourage him to stay undressed.

When he turned to her just seconds later he was the well-dressed, well-combed, slightly stiff-backed special emissary she had travelled with from Dakar.

"Will you join me in some breakfast?" he said hospitably. "Mine's on its way. At least, I hope it is."

"Oh, no thank you," she said, still slightly flushed. "I shouldn't have burst in on you this way. But Ambassador Thurston wanted you to have these at once." Liz Ashton delved briskly into a ladylike briefcase not much bigger than her trim pocketbook. "Some dispatches came in while we were on our way into town, quite urgent and highly confidential. I thought it best to bring them to you myself. They're about..."

"Dispatches before breakfast?" Nick interrupted, crossing over to her. "I couldn't look one in the eye. Do you know the song, 'How do you like your eggs? I like mine with a kiss'? Well, that's my position exactly. And if we're going to be working together, we should lose no time in getting acquainted." He put his hands lightly on her shoulders and bent his head over hers. She started back, her eyes shocked and incredulous.

"Why...!"

"Hush," he whispered into her ear, enjoying the faint whiff of perfume. "Be careful what you say. We're being overheard." He loosed a smacking kiss into the air just above her head. "The room is wired." Nick stepped back and patted her hand like an elderly cavalier. "Now I promise you I won't make another pass until...oh, at least until I've had my coffee. Look. No hands." He spread them out palms upward and grinned at her.

"Why, Mr. Carter! You surprise me." Liz said with mock severity, and a new look of comprehension in her eyes.

"It's just that you look so charming," he said earnestly. "I couldn't help myself. And I can't stand business before breakfast."

"What would you have done if Ambassador Thurston had brought the reports over himself?" she asked, smiling. "Or sent Tad Fergus?"

"Well, certainly not *that*," Nick said emphatically. "I know people say unkind things about the State Department, but they're really not true at all—most of them."

Liz laughed. She had dimples, Nick noted approvingly, and the soft but distinct laugh lines of an attractive young woman who often found life funny and didn't care who knew it. "Well, some of them obviously are. I take it you don't want these things, then?" she patted her briefcase enquiringly.

Nick sighed. "I hadn't planned to start work nearly so soon. But you might as well go ahead and give them to me; I'll have a quick look."

She placed a thick sealed envelope into his out-stretched hand. Opening it, he found a report from "our man in Morocco," a freshly compiled list of recent local happenings, and a coded cable from Hawk. Liz watched with a slightly quizzical expression as he drew the cable from its dull-red wrapper. She knew the colour meant Top Secret, For Your Eyes Only, and that the contents must be highly classified intelligence matters. It seemed strange to her that he could be so casual about it all.

But it was only his surface manner that was casual. Hawk's message read:

ACTION IVAN REVISES EARLY ESTIMATE WITH TRUE APPRAISAL ORIGINAL FAKES NOT RED WHITE AND BLUE BUT RED WITH WIDE YELLOW STRIPE ITEM DOUBLECHECK LOCAL TEAM PROVES TRUE BLUE FOR USE ITEM URGE CONSIDER WHITE HOUSE LEAD.

Nick's brows drew together. Most of it was obvious enough. "Action Ivan" referred to the AXE contact in the Kremlin. Agent P-4 had gained access to the original of Rubitchev's report on the bomb fragments found after the Nyanga explosions. They were not American, as Polikov had claimed, but Red Chinese. Obviously the Russian delegate had lied to cover up the growing rift between the two titans of Communism. The "local team" of American officials—and that included Liz—had been checked out again by the AXE Snoop Group and found loyal and reliable beyond all reasonable doubt. But "White House lead"? That meant Casablanca, not the U.S. President. Nick glanced quickly at the Moroccan report.

Translated from AXE-talk into English, it complained bitterly about the impossibility of one man being able to report adequately on a city the size of Casablanca. But the writer *could* say that he'd noted a definite increase in the amount of Oriental shipping touching at Casa and the large number of recent narcotics cases. He ended with the usual plea for an assistant.

Nick smiled to himself at the familiar scream for help and swiftly skimmed the local data sheet. An isolated farmhouse attacked. A mysterious explosion in a grain storehouse. A riverboat stolen by an armed mob. His smile vanished.

He rose abruptly and reached for the one desk drawer that had a sturdy lock and key.

"That does it," he said crisply. "That tells me just about all I need to know." He made great play of opening, shutting and locking the drawer, and thrust the papers into his pocket. "I'll leave them here for the time being."

Liz watched him with her mouth open.

"But . . ." she began.

"Oh, don't worry," he said confidently. "They'll be safe enough. Tell me this—is there a café or a réstaurant around here called the Croix du Nord?"

He knew very well that there was. He'd done his home work well.

"Why, yes," she said, bewildered.

"Ah! So it does mean that," he announced with satisfaction. "I'm to be there at twelve o'clock today. With the least bit of luck I'll have the last piece of the puzzle in my hands before my lunchtime meeting with Makombe."

Which was nonsense, and he knew it. But what was the use of having a bugged room if you didn't put the bugs to work?

He winked at her. She closed her mouth and gave a shrug of resignation. Maybe he really did know what he was doing.

A heavy hand thundered at his bedroom door.

"Ah! Breakfast," he exclaimed. "At last." Moving to the door in long-legged, athletic strides, he stepped to one side before throwing it open.

An immense uniformed policeman, buttons gleaming and great muscles bulging beneath the neat khaki tunic stood on the landing and literally filled the doorway. He was a good six and a half-feet tall, Nick judged, feeling almost puny, and his blue-black face looked like the business end of a battering ram. One vast hand touched the forehead in a crisp salute.

Goliath spoke.

"The Honorable Mr. Carter?" The giant's voice was music.

Nick nodded. Liz, he could see, recognized the larger-than-lifesize apparition.

"The name's Carter," he admitted.

The saluting arm described a snappy downward swing that would have dropped an ox if there had been one in its way. Two horseshoe-sized heels snapped together. Now that the doorway was somewhat less than completely blocked. Nick became aware of a second man.

"Corporal Temba at your service, sir," said the incredibly dulcet tones. "Chief of Police Abe Jefferson begs your indulgence, sir."

"Abe Jefferson?" Nick repeated involuntarily, and stared into the passage for what he thought could only be another unbelievable being.

Corporal Temba stepped smartly and silently aside. The second man stepped into view.

He was about half Temba's size and was dressed like an ad for a Saville Row suit. His brown, young-old face reminded Nick of a good-humoured and highly intelligent monkey. But there was more than intelligence and humour in the penetrating eyes. It was too soon to tell exactly what it was, but it was something that reminded Nick partly of Hawk at his most perceptive and partly of his onetime friend and fellow agent Joe O'Brien who had died laughing. Laughing, because he had misled his torturers magnificently; and died, because they had found out in time to take revenge.

Chief Jefferson had a faint smile at the corners of his lips. But for the rest his face was grave. He nodded to Nick and bowed to Liz.

"Mr. Carter, sir. Miss Ashton."

"Come in Chief," said Nick. "Formal call, or something special?"

Jefferson shook his head regretfully. "I have to ask you to accompany me, Mr. Carter. No, I will not come in. I should like very much to talk to you, another time. But a most shocking thing has happened, and I have an urgent request for your immediate presence."

Liz turned pale and got up from her straight-backed chair.

"Whose request?" said Nick, his eyes flickering around the room to be sure that he could leave it unattended on a moment's notice.

"President Makombe's," Jefferson said quietly. "He has been shot. They will have to operate immediately. But he demanded to speak to you first. You will come at once?"

Nick heard Liz's swift intake of breath.

"Of course I will," he said quickly. "You have a car?"

The Chief nodded. "Please go ahead. I must be sure I have secured all my papers before leaving. You will understand, I'm sure."

They seemed to understand, because they backed tactfully out of the room and headed down the corridor. Nick could hear Liz say:

"*Shot!* Surely it was an accident."

Jefferson must have shaken his head, because the next thing Nick heard was Liz asking: "Does the Ambassador know? May I come along?"

Jefferson's answer was inaudible. Nick secured the hidden inside pocket containing all the documents relating to him and his work and dropped Pierre into his usual resting place. He could hear Liz's high heels going down the one flight of stairs to the lobby floor, but the conversation seemed to have come to an end. Possibly Jefferson had told her to button her lip while walking in a public place. Hugo slid neatly into his sheath and Wilhelmina snuggled comfortably into her special bed at the waistband of his trousers. His luggage was completely innocent, for once, as an honest diplomat's should be. Of course, there was that flat secret compartment to hold whatever documents he might want to hide, but he might as well give the lurking enemy a chance to find—or overlook—it before he used it as a hiding place. The lock on the desk drawer wasn't at all bad. They'd have to use some force to get it open.

He picked up his cane and left his room, locking the door behind him.

The long, closed car was waiting. Liz and Jefferson sat together in the back. The chauffeur stared unblinkingly ahead like a carved ebony statue, and Corporal Temba waited with his hamlike right hand on the back door handle.

It could be some kind of trap, of course, even though Liz had recognized these men. Nick chewed briskly on the thought and then dismissed it. Being spied upon was one thing; being abducted was another. And he'd done nothing to deserve it. Yet.

He got stiffly into the back seat. Temba slammed the door.

"In, Stonewall. Let us be on our way."

The massive corporal saluted and took his place in the front seat. Nick's eyebrows rose, Stonewall, yet.

"Hospital Dos Estrangeiros, Uru," Jefferson instructed. "Keep the foot upon the accelerator and the eye upon the traffic."

The ebony chauffeur nodded silently and shot breathtakingly into the swiftly moving stream of cars and military vehicles. Nick took note of them, as well as of the signs and names that characterized this fantastically polyglot young city. Portuguese, French, English, Nyangese and several tribal tongues were equally in evidence. Even American, it seemed, still had some sort of place. And no doubt he'd be encountering resentment in Russian before his stay was over.

"How is he?" asked Nick. "What happened?"

"The President is in extremely serious condition," Jefferson said quietly. "He is at present receiving treatment preparatory to the operation. A single bullet from what appears to have been a high-powered American rifle is lodged in his chest. It seems to have at least creased the heart, and has considerably damaged the lungs. I would say the situation is critical. He was shot when he stepped out of his office into the courtyard for a breath of air. You know the Presidential quarters used to be an old Portuguese fort?" Nick nodded. "One would naturally think of it as well-guarded by walls. if not by people." Jefferson's voice was bitter. "He was too confident, though. Too sure that *he* was not the target for all these attacks. Political target, perhaps, but not a murder victim. So he refused to have an adequate bodyguard. The gunman wounded a sentry at the gate and got away. The Army and the Police are both looking for him."

"Have you made any arrests in connection with previous events?" asked Nick.

Jefferson nodded. Their car swooped across an intersection and threw itself towards a traffic circle. The tyres screeched angrily but took them safely on to a broad, tree-lined highway leading out of the city. "Yes. Six arrests. One accidental death due to frenzy caused by overuse of hemp. One suicide. Two who produced a dozen witnesses to say they were fifty miles away from the scene of the crime . . ." Jefferson's lips curled. "And two who were so drug-ridden that they did not appear to know where they were—they were in jail—or what they'd done. And of course the Army has rounded up a number of prisoners in connection with the attacks on white settlements. They will say nothing. Nothing at all."

"So nobody talks," said Nick. "Not even to pass the buck—or cast the blame."

"That is correct. Not one of them will speak. But memory talks," Chief Jefferson said obscurely. "We are here."

The car swerved into a wide driveway and stopped in front of a pleasant, low-slung white building.

Liz and Chief Jefferson waited in the sunny reception room while Dr. Ngoma took Nick Carter up to the secluded suite on the second floor.

"For one moment only," he warned emphatically. "I would not have allowed this at all if the President had not insisted. I must urge you to receive his message, talk as little as possible, and leave at once. He is in the gravest danger."

Nick inclined his head. "I understand. I am only here to listen. Is there anything I can do to help?"

The young doctor shook his head. "Just be quick; that is all I ask."

President Makombe lay like a graven image amongst the white sheets, tubes clutching at his limbs like suckers at a rosebush. A strikingly handsome young man with a troubled face stood at his bedside. Nick looked down at the prone man and his agony. Rage and sympathy surged within him.

"President Makombe," he said, his voice low but firm. "Carter. My deepest regrets that we should have to meet this way."

Makombe's eyes fluttered open.

"Carter . . . And mine. I had to see you. And I had to

tell you this." He coughed painfully, and the young man at his bedside drew in a sharp breath and touched his shoulder gently. "This . . . ultimatum comes too soon. You must . . . You must work quickly." He closed his eyes for a moment, then forced them open with a visible effort. Nick stared down at the pained face on the pillow. The dull eyes looked back at him. "Whether I live or die," the voice said, "my country's future is in your hands. And all of Africa could be at stake. You must prove . . . you must prove . . ." The voice trailed off, and then began again. "It is up to you to find out who is doing these things. When I am better I will work with you. But now I cannot. My brother Rufus . . ." the dark head turned and faced the troubled young man. "My brother will help you. He knows all my affairs. He is not much interested in matters of state . . . but he is . . . aware . . ." The agonized eyes looked directly into Nick's. "I had . . . much more to say. But somehow . . . I think you know. I found out . . . today . . . it is . . . not so obvious as I thought. Or perhaps too obvious." The head lolled. "Rufus . . . be of help."

Julian Makombe's eyes closed.

Nick heard his own swift intake of breath and stepped back swiftly from the bed. Dr. Ngoma stepped forward and took the President's hand.

"Go now, both of you," he ordered sharply. "Yes, yes. he's still alive. But get out of here!" He bent over the leader of his country, oblivious to the two men quietly leaving the shadowed room.

Rufus Makombe plunged out into the sunlight like a man wrenching himself from a nightmare. Nick stood behind him on the hospital porch, half-hearing the call of the wild birds that reminded him of Kenya and half-seeing the brilliance of the extravagant flowers that thrust their way through the vines that lovingly entwined themselves about the huge, gnarled trees.

Jefferson and Liz walked quietly past them towards the waiting car. Nick turned to Rufus Makombe, searching for the right words to say to a man whose brother was the President of his country and a man whose brother was so close to death by the bullet of an assassin. But he stopped before he started.

The look that Rufus Makombe turned upon him was one of absolute hatred.

"He still thinks there can be some other explanation," he said very softly, his handsome face working. "But I do not. What is clear, is clear." His hot eyes bored into Nick's. "As long as he says I must help you, so I will. But I will tell you this: Only the gods themselves can help you if my brother dies."

MYSTERIOUS AFRICA

SUFUS MAKOMBE's sports car preceded them to the city, buzzing shrilly like an outraged bee. He had not stopped to waste insincere courtesies on anyone. The roar of his exhaust was like a slap in the face.

The Police Chief's car made its way back to town more sedately. Nick had time to fill in the details missing from his first hasty survey of the troubled town. There had been armed guards and military vehicles at the hospital. Now he saw them everywhere. Hard-faced, uniformed men sat poised on throbbing motorcycles at the roadside, as if waiting for the starter's signal. Armed men patrolled on foot. A convoy of jeeps passed them on the highway, heading out of town towards the hilly north.

Chief Jefferson sat in the front seat murmuring quietly into a two-way radio. Liz stared out of the window away from Nick, her lovely face pinched into a frown. Now that the sun had climbed past ten o'clock the day was hot and bright and the light almost harsh in its incredible clarity. The birds still sang as though they had something to be happy about and the air was fragrant with the warm scent of leaves and honeyed flowers in the sun. But there was something ominous in the very intensity of the light and the wild sweetness of the birdsong. The shadows appeared all the darker and the sound of marching feet and barked command all the more incongruous and unwelcome.

Jefferson clicked off his radio mike and turned to Nick. "Government House?"

Nick shook his head. "This afternoon. As part of a general tour. I'll have to send my respects to Vice-President Adebe, I expect, and then make arrangements with young Makombe for a car and some introductions.

"I'll supply the car," said Jefferson. "In fact, if you will permit the suggestion you may find it more satisfactory to put all your requests to me until Rufus Makombe is more himself." His dark monkey-face was pleasant but inscrutable. "It is understandable that he is extremely distressed right now and is not concerned with the amenities. I shall be honoured to assist you in any way I can."

Nick smiled faintly. "You should have been the diplomat," he commented. "May I ask why you don't seem to share the prevailing resentment towards Americans in general and me in particular? Is it because your job demands that you keep an open mind, or has it something to do with your name?"

Abe Jefferson bared white, perfect teeth in a companionable grin. "Both. And more. I would gain nothing for my country by antagonizing you, whether or not the United States is behind all these frightful crimes. And then I have to admit that I am slightly prejudiced in America's favour. I was brought up by an American family, on their farm about two hundred miles south of here. They taught me everything they could, from how to wash behind my ears to how to listen to music. Somewhere along the way they let me choose a name for myself. I'd lost my own, you see." He said casually, as though losing one's name was an everyday sort of thing requiring no explanation. "We were doing history at the time. Otherwise you might have come to Africa to meet Huck Finn or Davy Crockett. Oh . . . by the way—slow down, Uru—that's the Russian embassy."

He pointed out of the right-hand window. Nick saw a mess of jagged walls and fallen brick. Torn trees thrust their raw branches through spaces that had once been windows. A piece of roof hung crazily over part of the front wall like a flap of torn and bleeding scalp. The rest of it had either crashed down inside the building or been blown to powder. Two soldiers stood watch over the ruins. But there was little left that needed watching.

"Two people were killed in that one," said Liz, and her voice cracked. "It's a miracle that it wasn't any worse."

Nick grunted agreement. "Pick up anyone for that, Chief?"

Jefferson shook his head. "No one even saw anyone. We think it was a time fuse. Could have been planted by any messenger or tradesman or repairman."

"How about our Embassy? In anything like that shape?"

Liz answered. "Not quite that bad, but bad enough. The living quarters held up pretty well, and it happened over the weekend so no one was in the offices. Good thing, too, because they were wrecked."

"I'd like that car for this afternoon, Chief," Nick said thoughtfully. "And your presence too, if you can make it. My hotel at two o'clock?"

"Without fail," nodded Jefferson.

"And something else," said Nick. "I'm going to be at the Café Croix du Nord at noon. Uh . . . at the risk of stepping on someone's toes, may I talk freely?"

"Absolutely." Jefferson's nod was emphatic. "Stonewall and Uru are more than staff. They are trusted friends."

"Good." Nick pulled thoughtfully at his ear, a habit he had caught from Hawk. Liz watched him, thinking to herself that he had very finely shaped ears. And a strong, decisive chin. Not to mention the almost godlike nose. And piercing eyes that could look hard as steel one moment and be filled with laughter the next. And beautifully muscular chest and shoulders... Down, girl, she told herself. These lonesome travellers with kiss appeal always turned out to have a wife and six or seven children.

"I'd like a messenger," said Nick, pleasantly conscious of her scrutiny. "Someone you can trust, who isn't known to be associated with you. I'll be at a table near the door, conspicuously waiting for someone. Getting nervous and looking at my watch, because your man's a little late. Have him there at about ten minutes past twelve, and let him bring me a verbal message of some kind. I don't care what it is, just so long as he's properly secretive and gives the impression that he's bringing me information of immense significance. I'll talk to him for a few minutes and then give him his cue to leave. Do you have anyone who can play a role like that? It's particularly important that he should look capable of . . . let's say, selling information, and yet be completely trustworthy. Also, as I said, that he has no known connection with you."

Jefferson thought for a moment and then grinned suddenly. "I have a friend visiting me from Cairo. He is the gentlest, most honest man in the world, and I would trust him with my last sou if he were starving, but he is afflicted with a most sinister looking cast in his eye. He looks capable of the most appalling crimes. Yet he is decent and quick-witted and is known to no one in this part of the country. I am positive he will co-operate. You will be going to your hotel now? I will call you there and confirm the arrangement."

"Do that," said Nick, "bearing in mind that all the walls have ears. Or did you perhaps know that already?"

Jefferson stared at him. "Do they indeed?" he said at last. "No, I did not know that. I was not even aware which room was yours until I enquired of the desk clerk. Do you not wish to have the encumbrances removed?"

"Not yet," said Nick. "Not as long as they amuse me. Miss Ashton, may we drop you at your office? Oh, that's right. You don't have an office, do you? What sort of arrangements are there for me to meet the Ambassador?"

"In answer to your string of questions," she said, smiling. "No, please don't drop me. I have to talk to you on behalf of my boss—as his representative. You're going to have to put up with me until this afternoon, when he'll have got rid of some outraged Soviet visitors whom he doesn't want to inflict on you. One of my jobs is to keep them out of your hair. And yes, we do have an office, temporary quarters in the *Sun* building. There's a skeleton staff on duty. His name is Tad Fergus," she added.

Abe Jefferson chuckled. "Shocking, the way the emancipated female talks about the pursuant male. Ah, here we are."

Uru slid the big car to a stop alongside the kerb. Corporal Stonewall Temba leapt out and opened the kerb side rear door with a casual strength that nearly ripped it off its hinges. Nick's mouth twitched into a slight smile. He liked these people, all of them. He only hoped to God that he could trust them. But he would soon be sure of that, after today—and the small traps he had set.

Jefferson let Liz walk on ahead and did not speak again until he was out of earshot of all but Nick. Then he spoke very softly.

"I do not know, as yet, how much you care to say in front of others," he murmured. "Myself, I am sure of all these people. But if your room is wired, you must be very, very careful. Now." Once again he reminded Nick, fleetingly, of Hawk. "I shall speak to my friend. If he agrees, I will call and simply say 'The meeting is arranged.' If not, I will say, 'The meeting is postponed.' Agreed?"

Nick nodded. "Any other prospects if he falls through?"

"I will try to think of someone and let you know in time. There is one other thing that may be of help to you." Liz stopped at the entrance to the hotel and waited for them. Jefferson stopped as if about to turn back to the car. "The two addicts we are still holding in the jail. We knew at once that they are not from these parts. We find that they are known in Dakar, that they are common criminals with no political affiliations but who will do anything to support their vice. Of late they have been seen frequenting a back-street place in Dakar called The Hop Club." His expression reflected his distaste. "It is a gathering place for the beatniks of the new world, the worst type. Not poets drinking coffee, but the lost ones. Now I do not know how this can help you, but perhaps something will suggest itself to you."

"Something just may," Nick murmured. "Thanks. I'll hear from you, then."

He shook hands with Jefferson. Stonewall saluted mightily from his post beside the car.

Liz was tapping her foot impatiently at the hotel entrance.

"Secrets, already," she said disapprovingly as Nick joined her.

"Uh-huh," he agreed cheerfully. "I wanted to know what he meant by 'the pursuant male' in connection with Tad Fergus."

"Oh, really!" she protested. "Is that all you have to

think about?" A little pink spot appeared provocatively on each cheek.

"Of course not," Nick said reproachfully. "I'm also thinking it's about time I had some breakfast."

She stood watching him with that Men-Are-Impossible look on her face while he checked at the desk for messages or callers. Nothing had come in. They walked together up the one flight of stairs to what the management persisted in calling his first floor room and what all Americans think of as the second. Nick remembered to use his cane to help him up the stairs.

"Back injury?" Liz enquired sympathetically.

"Mm. Slipped in the bathtub as a lad," he lied.

He stopped outside Room 101, rear, and fished for his keys.

But the door was already unlocked.

Nick pushed Liz gently away from the door. "Stay back," he whispered urgently. With one long arm he thrust the door abruptly inward and waited.

Nothing happened.

A breeze from the open window fluttered the breakfast tablecloth on the service cart. Nick hefted his cane experimentally and glided silently into the room, his eyes darting about like pinpoint flashlights. The built-in geiger counter that was his sixth sense was sending him urgent warning signals. The desk drawer he had locked so carefully was open. A floorboared creaked faintly. Inside the closet? Sounded like it.

"Why, it was only the waiter," Liz said from behind him, relief and amusement in her voice. "He forgot to lock the door."

Nick cursed her silently and flung her a furious look.

"Sure," he said, as easily as he could. "Just wait outside for me, will you? I'll pick up the book and be right with you."

The closet door flung open even as he spoke and a black-and-white figure shot out, one arm raised and flashing forward with the suddenness of a bolt of lightning in a summer storm. Nick raised the cane like a shield and twisted his body sideways. He saw the flash of silver and heard the click of metal against the cane, and then he heard Liz scream.

What happened next was scarcely a credit to agent N-3, the man whose fellow agents called him Killmaster. He lost his legendary balance. And as he stumbled the flying figure snarled and flung itself full-tilt against the service cart. The metal table overturned and slammed down on Nick. Plates, coffee pot and scrambled eggs cascaded over him. He swore bitterly and fluently and made a wild grab for the bare black legs that streaked past him towards the window. His clutching fingers slid off a sleek greased surface and scrabbled at thin air. With a blistering oath that outdid all his previous efforts he gathered himself together and sprang at the black man whose long, greased legs were straddling the window sill. Nick grasped furiously at a pair of soiled white shorts and heard them tear. The man made a strange yelping sound and disappeared over the window sill, leaving Nick with his hands full of torn shorts and his face full of egg.

Below him, in the square, the man ran off with a curious hobbling gait. Clearly, he had hurt his leg on landing. Clearly, too, he was much concerned at pulling down his shirttails as far as they would go. The last Nick saw of him was a pair of frantically bobbing buttocks followed by a yapping dog.

Nick was grinning and cursing to himself when he heard Liz's half-sobbing giggle. Christ Almighty! He had forgotten all about her. He swung around, still clutching the foolishly torn pants, and saw Liz inside the room slumped against the wall. She was pointing feebly at him and shaking with weak laughter, even though tears of shock and pain trickled down her face.

"Oh, you look... you look so... you look so funny! And him!" She went off into gales of laughter. The blood spread inexorably across her left breast and oozed through the cloth of her dress in tiny globules.

"God *damn*!" Nick dropped the shorts and moved towards her, unaware that he was dripping with cold coffee. One hand slammed the door shut and the other went around her waist. *"I told you to stay outside!"*

She giggled again. "I wouldn't have missed it... for the

. . . world," she managed, and her eyes closed. She slumped into his arms.

Nick stood there for a long moment, just holding her and thinking dark thoughts about himself. The thrown knife, deflected by his cane, lay near the door where it had fallen after it had struck her. Special Emissary Carter's hotel room was an unholy mess. He called himself one last, unflattering name and hoisted Liz gently by the legs and shoulders and picked his way past the mess of overturned breakfast cart to the bed. He put her down as carefully as he would a sleeping child.

The wound, he soon saw, was more blood than serious damage. And Liz was far more woman than sleeping child. He slowed the bleeding with a damp towel and rummaged in the bureau for his flask. Two of his clean shirts were smudged with grease, he noted bitterly, and then reproached himself for even thinking of it while she lay there bleeding.

He uncapped the flask and poured a shot into the metal cup.

"Do I smell good Scotch?" she asked interestedly.

Nick turned. Liz was sitting up on the bed and clutching the towel to her well-rounded bosom. She was pale but in full control of herself.

"You do," he said, and made his way around the mess to give it to her.

She sipped and spluttered and the colour came back into her face.

"I'm sorry . . ." they began at once, and stopped.

Nick tried again. "I shouldn't have let you come back with me. I did, and I'm sorry. Now pull the top of that dress down and let me have a look—at the wound, of course."

She reached up obediently and let out a little gasp of pain.

"I can't do it with one hand. My God, look how its spreading! You'll have to help me take it off."

He fumbled cautiously with the small hook at the back. At last it loosened, and the short zipper slid down its appointed course.

"Can you stand up? I can't seem to get it off this

way." She nodded and rose shakily.

The dress got as far as her hips and stuck. Nick manoeuvered and tugged.

"For God's sake, how can you wear these tight things in this hot climate?" he grumbled.

"It's not tight. You just don't have the knack."

"Hmmph. I don't have the shape. Wiggle a bit, will you?" Liz wiggled. He tried not to notice how seductively her hips moved. "Now raise your right arm and try to get it out."

Liz concentrated for a moment.

"Okay. Now pull down," said Nick thoroughly engrossed in his task. Liz pulled. Nick tugged.

"There! That's one," he said triumphantly. "Now sit down and let me get it over your head."

There was silence but for their breathing and the rustle of cloth.

"Ah! That does it. Take it easy while I get the left arm out. This may hurt a bit."

"Yes, Doctor," she said bravely.

She winced only slightly as her left arm parted from the dress. The other sound was Nick's involuntary sigh of approval at her scantily clad form. Bloodstains and all, she was delectable in her half-slip and not much else. He was amazed at the magnificence of her high, full breasts, at the ripe but firm perfection of her body. Strange that he hadn't fully appreciated it before. Obviously her dress wasn't nearly tight enough.

She looked up into his eyes and saw him staring down at her alluring softness. Her right hand reached up and gently touched his face.

"What a way to have to start," she said ambiguously, and smiled. Her hand caressed his cheek. He put his own hand over hers and bent to kiss her lightly on the cheek. But somehow his lips found hers and lingered on them, and one hand stole around her back and stroked it soothingly.

She drew her lips away from him with a little gasp and he straightened up immediately. There was a compact first aid kit in his luggage and he made use of it. He cleansed and bound the wound with a light, quick touch, forcing his fingers to behave themselves and his eyes to attend to the business at hand. While he worked his mind reconstructed the hectic events of the last few minutes. Intruder entered via bedroom door. Opened window in readiness for rapid escape. Searched in obvious places, including locked desk drawer, found nothing. Luggage undamaged. Intruder anxious to make getaway, willing to kill and run rather than hang about and answer questions. Naturally.

It didn't prove a thing. The visit may have had nothing to do with whoever might be listening in. Nick wished he knew if the desk drawer had been opened first or last.

He helped Liz into the seersucker robe he usually forgot to wear himself and went into the bedroom for a rapid wash and change. When he rejoined her he was wearing clean trousers, a fresh shirt with a small grease smudge, and a calculating look. Liz lay back on the bed and watched him, feeling sensual and adventurous.

"I have to get you out of here," Nick said, "and put in a report on this crazy mess." For Chrissake, if he'd only removed that bugging mechanism before, he could have called Abe Jefferson and had him straighten this out in one swift, easy motion. But it was too obvious a thing to do just now; he'd have to leave it there. How would a genuine diplomat react? Flustered. Indignant. Ineffectual ... Fine, I'm doing fine, Nick told himself with bitter self-disgust. Show me a mouse, and I'll faint. He eyed Liz.

"Is there some woman friend you can call who can bring you a dress? I can't let you out of here looking like that."

"I have no women friends," Liz said with languid pride.

"Then what about Tad?"

The phone rang.

He scooped it up impatiently.

A muffled voice said distantly: "Carter?"

"Yes!" Nick snapped.

"The meeting is arranged," the voice said sepulchrally.

"Oh!" said Nick. The light dawned. "I'll be there." There was a click. Nick stood there holding the telephone. and a slow grin spread across his face. There he was. in the midst of an ungodly mess—throwing knife, toast and coffee, an ineffectual cane, an undressed girl with large breasts and a shoulder wound, and the memory of a greasy would-be killer with no pants. What he needed more than anything in the world was an honest cop. And here he stood, a telephone in his hand and an honest police chief at the other end. And he couldn't say a word. It would screw up his whole undercover deal with his friend, the honest cop.

He looked at Liz and slowly replaced the receiver. A score of pictures tumbled through his mind, of the Africa he had adventured through not so many years before. Of the wild journey through the bush, the trumpeting of the great bull elephants, the chanting of the red-eyed woman witchdoctor, the hideous rituals of the leopard men, the eerie stillness of the dripping forests and the sudden animal screams. Mysterious Africa... with not a single bottle-opener in the bathroom. And now? A wild jumble of conflicting politics and bomb fragments and bugs that didn't wiggle through the beds but listened in on conversations. Intrigue in high places and sinister visitors in search of documents. He shook his head. In some ways this new-old continent was even more mysterious than before. Nick glanced at his watch. After eleven. "The meeting is arranged."

He'd have to hurry. He reached again for the inquisitive telephone.

THE COCKEYED OPTIMIST

"Try to get hold of a *what* for Miss Ashton?" Abe Jefferson's voice was incredulous, It had taken some time before the Police Chief could be reached on the telephone. Apparently he had been thoughtful enough to place his mystery call from somewhere other than his office. During that time Nick had been able to think himself into the person of an enraged, bewildered diplomat and prepare a carefully guarded story that would fit in with an eavesdropper's version of what had happened in Special Emissary Carter's room.

"A dress," Nick repeated patiently. "I'll explain it all

when you get here. But she can't go around in her ..."

"I shop at the Paris Boutique," Liz called out helpfully. "They know my size and everything."

Nick relayed the information.

Jefferson chuckled. "I'll ask my wife to take care of this, or I'll never hear the end of it. In the meantime I'll be on my way."

He was there with his estimable Corporal in a matter of minutes. His face was a kaleidoscope of expressions as he stared around the room. Liz sat on the edge of the bed clutching Nick's bathrobe to her ample bosom and trying to look demure. With her long, dark hair falling loosely about her shoulders and the robe revealing lengths of lovely leg and her eyes sparkling with Scotch and excitement, she looked anything but. The overturned service cart, instead of suggesting a brush with death, only contributed to the general impression of an uninhibited romp.

"Well!" Jefferson remarked appraisingly. "It must have been quite a party!"

"It was nothing of the sort, said Nick severely. "It was a shocking experience. If that fellow isn't picked up ..."

"He already has been," said Jefferson, his lips twitching. "Charged with indecent exposure and being improperly clad in public."

Liz giggled. "I'll be next."

The soohing cadence of Corporal Stonewall Temba's voice rippled across the room. "Chief Jefferson, sir. Mr. Carter, sir. Are you aware that there are listening devices implanted in this room?"

Nick turned and stared at the massive African with the mellifluous voice. Chief Jefferson smiled benignly.

"No, really?" said Nick at last, acid thinning his voice. "Then I suggest that you find out at once who is responsible for this further outrage ..."

"Remove them, Corporal," Jefferson said crisply.

Stonewall's huge hands clawed at the wall and something snapped decisively. A loose wire dangled from the ceiling. "Done, sir," he boomed melodiously. "Perhaps, also, the telephone." He lifted the instrument between vast thumb and massive forefinger and plucked at something beneath the base. "Excuse me now."

He wafted swiftly from the room like some storybook genie and closed the door silently behind him.

"I had hoped," Nick said carefully, fixing Jefferson with a stony stare, "to catch the eavesdropper in the act. But now, my friend, you've blown it."

"Not necessarily, Mr. Carter." Jefferson picked up the intruder's throwing knife by the tip and viewed it thoughtfully. "You told us about it you know. And we prepared ourselves. Oh, I realize what you intended." He raised a placating hand. "But you must not forget that I *am* the Chief of Police, and I must handle these things in my own way." His monkey face was serious, and the sharp eyes held assurance and command. "You have your job, sir, and I have mine. Now suppose you tell me just what happened."

Nick scanned his face and made a rapid assessment. If this was round two, he'd lost two in a row without throwing a punch. But he liked what he saw in Jefferson's face, and perhaps it was just as well that he could talk in front of these two people without wondering who else was listening in.

"Right," he said. "Sit down. I called you because I think Miss Ashton may be in danger if she stays here. And as you know I have to leave in a few minutes. What happened was this..."

In a few crisp phrases he sketched the details. Abe Jefferson frowned and smiled alternately.

"What I would like you to do," Nick wrapped up his story, "is square this with the hotel people—I don't want to hang around explaining things to them—and take care of the lady for me. And of course try to sweat something out of the fellow with the bare behind. Who sent him, what for, how his orders—well. As you said, you're the Chief." It was the first time in years that Nick had spoken freely to a policeman, and it made him feel wildly indiscreet and slightly hamstrung at the same time. "By the way, is the meeting still arranged?"

Jefferson nodded. "Oh, yes. There was no need to interfere with that. You must not worry, Mr. Carter. I shall not get in your way." His lively eyes probed at Nick's face. "I will only intrude myself when I am sure there is police business to be done. Catching wiretappers, protecting undraped ladies, and the like." His face crinkled. "Even in those somewhat specialised areas I shall endeavour to be less a hindrance than a help. The attention you are attracting is of much interest to me. We can be of mutual value."

"I hope so," Carter said sincerely. "Any word from the hospital?"

"The President is holding his own," the Chief said quietly. "That is all we know. We have not yet made the news public. There is a danger of anti-American demonstrations—like the retaliatory bombing of the American Embassy."

"Is that what you think it was?" Liz spoke up unexpectedly. "I don't think so."

Nick flashed her an approving look.

"I'd like to hear more from you later on, when you're decently dressed and we have some time," he told her. "Chief, you'll see that she gets home, will you? I'll have to be on my way. Meet you in the lobby at two?"

Jefferson nodded. "If not myself, then Stonewall. He and Uru will take you wherever you wish to go."

"See you later," Liz murmured comfortably. "Perhaps we can have breakfast together some time this afternoon."

Nick walked swiftly down the broad main street and consulted his mental map. The Croix du Nord was four blocks south and three to the west on a broad thoroughfare in the business district. His cane tapped rhythmically along the smooth sidewalk and across the streets thinly speckled with traffic. The town was oddly silent—he could hear with separate clarity each swish of tyres and each honk of a horn and each pedlar's call. There was something ominous about it, as if the town had stilled its normal sounds to listen. Or wait. Or watch. He wondered if the news about Makombe had somehow managed to leak out, or if it was just that he was not yet attuned to the natural quietness of an African city. Abimako, after all, was not New York.

And yet it was big enough to support a stunning array of adolescent skyscrapers and a downtown section of unrivalled department stores and restaurants flanked by markets ablaze with brilliant colour and usually frenetically busy. No, the quiet tension was real, almost real enough to touch.

Nick detoured suddenly from his appointed course and strode swiftly into the newly completed railroad station. The morning's dispatches were burning a hole in his inside pocket and there was no knowing what the rest of the day would bring. He found the men's toilets and made himself at home in one of them. When he had mentally photographed the contents of the papers he tore them into miniscule pieces and flushed them into oblivion. Then he left the station and made his way briskly to the Café Croix du Nord.

It was five minutes to twelve when he sat down at a sidewalk table near the door and ordered a cup of Nyanga's thick, strong coffee and an apéritif. After a few minutes of nervous sipping and watch-glancing he walked into the café and bought himself a pack of Players at an exorbitant price. He peeled it open while his eyes grew accustomed to the comparative gloom and lit one as he glanced casually around.

He knew even before his eyes told him that one of his visitors had already arrived, because little snakes seemed to be slithering down his back. The man with the unhealthy green face was sitting at a corner table half-hidden in the shadows, studiously not watching him. But his view of Nick's chosen table was perfect.

Nick walked back into the sunlight and sat down. Five past twelve. He scanned the sidewalk with what he hoped looked like controlled eagerness.

An unusual number of soldiers and police constables mingled with the brightly robed figures who were passing by. A beggar with shrivelled arms stopped at his table with his outstretched hands. Nick shook his head sternly and turned his face away. The man whined and shuffled off.

At a few seconds before ten past twelve a tall man with hunched shoulders walked slowly past the café and turned back. He ignored the one free table and came over to Nick in a curious sideways shamble, and the face that darted about suspiciously was one that would have been conspicious for its villainy even in an Arab bazaar. The cast in his eye, the cruelly curved thin lips and the dingy, pitted skin all added up to a picture of unbelievable malevolence.

He sidled closer to Nick.

"Feelthy pictures?" he hissed.

"Later, perhaps," Nick muttered. "Got anything else?"

"A question. You are Carter?" One surprisingly limpid eye stared down at Nick. The other went off on a trip of its own.

"Uh-huh. You have a message?"

The newcomer nodded. "From Cousin Abe." He glanced around furtively. "Are we alone?"

"We are surrounded. Sit down and hiss me a message of great import, stopping only to demand money in the middle of it. But tell me first what I can call you."

"You can call me Hakim, because that is my name. And you will have to plot the moves for me because I am new at this sort of thing."

He pulled up a chair and sat down close to Nick, contriving by his manner to suggest some hideous conspiracy. The back of his head faced the watcher in the café. His unmatched eyes struggled valiantly to peer at Nick.

"I have been sent by my superiors to bring you news that the enemy would give their balls to hear," he said darkly. "But I am not a ball-collector and therefore I have come to you. You must understand, though, that the information has great value. I cannot speak until I have your promise to pay my price." He leered horribly at Nick.

Nick frowned and shook his head.

"I refuse to be intimidated," he said coldly. "You may frighten me to death with that ferocious leer, but your demands will get you nowhere. My Government has instructed me to lose my virtue rather than their money."

"Then buy me a drink, at least," Hakim said threateningly.

"I do not buy drinks for informers," Nick answered stuffily.

Hakim pushed back his chair. "I do not inform unless I drink."

"All right, all right, stay where you are. Why didn't

Abe warn me you're a blackmailer?" Nick signalled a waiter. "Better order for yourself. I'd feel shy, asking them for human blood."

Hakim ordered a double shot of an ill-reputed local painkiller.

"I hate the stuff," he confided after the waiter had looked at him with loathing and gone back to the bar. "But I feel it fits the part."

"What do you actually do for a living?" Nick asked curiously.

"How nice of you to put it that way. Many people ask me—'What did you do when you were alive?' Unkind, are they not? I teach. In fact, I am a professor at the University of Cairo, God help them."

"What do you teach? Medieval Eastern Torture?"

The incredible face split into an even more incredibly attractive grin. "I call my course The Seven Lively Arts."

His drink came. Hakim threw back his head and swallowed.

"Now the message?" he asked, his shoulders hunching suggestively.

"Now the message," Nick agreed.

Hakim talked. His eyes flickered off in impossible directions and his evil-looking head bent low like a striking snake. Beyond him, in the café, the man with the froggy lids fidgeted impatiently. Hakim talked of his long friendship with Abe Jefferson and of the promising students in his course—all the while hissing and crooning in an astonishingly evil way that gave the impression of a grasping man acting as a go-between for two extremely important principals. It was a masterly performance.

Nick cut him off at last.

"That'll do it. Now I have a message for you. First, though—I gather you can handle a tail. Are you willing to do it now? I warn you, it may be dangerous."

The awful eyes rolled lasciviously. "Time now for feelthy pictures?"

"Enough, Hakim." Nick kept himself from grinning. "Keep 'em for Cairo. This one is a little green-faced man, watching us right now. He's inside going crazy because he couldn't listen. Five foot six, globes for eyes with shutters over them, slightly handsomer than you but somehow much more horrible . . ."

"Unbelievable," hissed Hakim.

"Yeah, you'd think so. Now he may want to follow me, but I don't think so because he knows where he can find me. I want to follow *him*. So I give myself an opportunity. You. And I give him a reason, in case he doesn't already think he has one. I give you a message to take back. Take back where, I don't care. Shake him as soon as you can." Hakim cocked his head over one hunched shoulder while Nick reached into his pocket and drew out an envelope that contained nothing but a blank sheet of paper.

"Invisible writing?" Hakim suggested helpfully.

"Of course," Nick agreed. "A new, permanent process. I will now add something to it."

He wrote swiftly, inscribing a meaningless message in a meaningless cipher on the innocent sheet of paper.

"I feel something slimy on the back of my neck," Hakim murmured. "Is that the way it feels when he watches?"

Nick folded the paper and put it back in the envelope. He sealed it decisively and thrust it at Hakim.

"Be sure not to guard this with your life," he said. "Yes, that's the way it feels when he watches. And I thought *I* was being over-sensitive.'"

"Sickening," said Hakim, putting the envelope into his pocket. "I've felt this way only once before. And the fellow who was watching then turned out to be slightly more revolting than Jack the Ripper. He went for little boys."

Nick stared at him, surprised that anyone else could share his own inexplicable revulsion without even having seen the man they both meant.

"Well, we're not little boys. How long are you free from the University?"

"One week," Hakim answered. "If you're thinking of asking me to join you again in something like this, the answer is yes."

"Thanks," said Nick. "I was. I'll check with cousin Abe. Now get lost. Literally."

Hakim pushed back his chair. "You don't think you should give me money?"

"I do not," Nick said firmly. "You might keep it, for one thing. For another, I don't want to get you mugged for money. Let's not cloud the issue. Go lose yourself. I have dates for this afternoon."

"A pox on you and all your dates," Hakim growled sullenly, pushing back his chair. "Thank you for your lousy drink."

He sidled away without a backward glance. Nick watched him for a moment with apparent distaste and then let himself sink deep into thought.

When the man who made snakes slither down Nick's spine sauntered on to the sidewalk and strolled off after Hakim, Nick was staring thoughtfully into space and drumming his fingers on the tabletop. Nick let him walk as far as the crosswalk before he placed a bill and some change on the table and slowly started after him.

Nick crossed to the far side of the street and paused for a moment at the window of a curio shop. Hakim's tall figure was two blocks away and moving with surprising speed in spite of the shambling gait. His follower stayed well behind him. But the man's short legs made sudden little toddling movements as if he had underestimated Hakim's walking pace and had to hurry to keep him in sight.

When Nick moved away from the curio shop window, a tall, coal-black man on the café side of the street matched his movements and glided along the opposite sidewalk with aloof dignity. Nick stopped on the corner to buy a paper from a newsboy. Hakim had gained a block and the short man was holding his distance behind him. The tall black man, in filmy cloak and full trousers pinched at the ankle, stopped on his corner and waited for nothing in particular. Nick walked on. So did the man in the cloak.

It could be coincidence.

Nick looked at his watch and increased his speed. Two minutes later he was crossing a small square only yards behind the green-face man. He lost Hakim momentarily but saw him again beyond the trees. The man in the cloak was closing in.

Hakim sauntered into a narrow street and turned into one that was even narrower. Here were lowslung dwelling places with huge brass doorknobs that had once been a symbol of status but now were covered with grime and neglect. Narrow steps led down into dim little basement-level shops smelling of old leather and overripe fruit. The cobbled road curved crazily and Nick paused to let the man with the green face get ahead. The cloaked black man passed him and stopped to peer into a window that had nothing in it but a dying potted plant.

Nick moved. He moved. It was not coincidence.

Both Hakim and his follower were out of sight. Nick rounded the curve and walked rapidly down an uneven slope. Once-white steps led up on one side to houses that desperately needed a coat of paint and down on the other to ramshackle wooden buildings that looked like abandoned storehouses.

The man with the sick green face was standing in the middle of a narrow footpath with his hands dangling at his sides. Even from the back he looked puzzled and betrayed. Hakim was nowhere in sight.

His disappearance was as skilfully contrived as his appearance. And even more astonishing.

Nick shot a sideways glance at his own black shadow and decided that the time had come to say goodbye. And he was adept in the art of vanishing himself. The cloaked man gave him just the fraction of time he needed by stopping like a statue and staring at Green Face, who obligingly gave him something to look at by stamping his foot down on the half-paved path and swaying like a man with a fever. Nick glided quietly into a doorway and turned a knob that yielded to his touch. He was not worried about finding the battered building occupied; he knew with cynical certainty that in this forlorn part of town he would be able to buy his way in or out of anything.

The room smelled vile. A snoring man lay on a pile of newspapers in the corner and told the world through his nostrils that he didn't give a damn who came or went or lived or died. A rickety ladder led upstairs to a loft. Nick took the steps quickly, still ready with explanations and defences. But the loft had long ago been abandoned to the mice.

He looked through the grimy broken window at the scene below. A donkey cart was making its thoughtful way down the lopsided slope, its driver nodding sleepily in the noonday sun. The man with the green face had recovered himself and was walking purposefully along the shack-lined footpath (where Hakim had somehow staged his disappearing act) looking into every impossible little nook and cranny. The black man with the cloak had walked back to the curve of the cobbled road and was looking around wildly as if his pocket had been picked. Then he came back down the slope and peered anxiously along Green Face's footpath. Green Face was temporarily out of sight, but Nick could predict where he would re-appear. The Cloak started along the footpath.

Nick whistled shrilly. The Cloak froze in his tracks. Nick whistled again, urgently. The tall African swung around and started walking slowly towards Nick's hiding place. Nick kept on encouraging him with urgent little whistles. In the distance he watched Green Face emerge from an alley and walk on. Down below, the African ambled cautiously up to the doorway Nick had entered moments before.

Now! thought Nick, and raised his cane. Damn, the angle was too sharp. The African disappeared from his view and the door below Nick opened.

He was waiting at the opening of the loft even before the African took his first cautious step into the room. When the flowing white cloak came into view, Nick aimed his unfamiliar new weapon and fired.

The man in the cloak gave a yelp of pain and clutched his shoulder. He swayed for a moment, his face contorted more with surprise than pain. And then he dropped.

Nick looked out of the broken window. Green Face was coming back.

THE flowing clothes concealed nothing but a short stabbing knife, some crumpled Nyangese notes and a set of rather gaudy underwear. Nick left the tall man where he had fallen and peered out through the partly open door. Hakim's follower had left the footpath and was standing near the curve of the uneven roadway. His shuttered eyes roamed back and forth along the street and found nothing that pleased them. He could see Nick's open door, but he could not possibly know its significance. There were other open doors on that shabby little street.

Not once had he looked back while trailing Hakim. Probably he had relied on the second man to guard his rear, or else he had not even thought of being followed and had intended to use the cloaked man as a substitute shadow in case Hakim had spotted him. But whatever he'd intended hadn't worked. His face was a study in bafflement.

Nick watched him standing there looking impotent and angry and saw him purse his lips into a whistle. A fluting sound hung on the air and faded. He waited, tried again. Two small children and a mangy mongrel bounded down the slope to investigate. The dog barked. The children turned and ran.

The man stood there for another moment and then turned and walked slowly back in the direction from which the trailing procession had come.

Nick left the snoring stranger and the unconscious one, thinking to himself what a nice chat they could have when they woke up, and glided like a phantom after the man with the green face.

At first it was about as tricky as Nick had thought it would be. His quarry stopped at every shadow and started at every sound. Once in a while he would swing about and stare up the street behind him, his head darting about in little searching motions. Now and then he stopped on a corner and whistled hopefully, as though he thought the man in the cloak might have turned up the wrong narrow street and was waiting to be found. Nick cursed his conspicuously American clothes and the telltale cane, and dodged and hung back until he felt sure he would lose his man.

But then, unaccountably, the man quickened his pace and gave up his futile search. He walked rapidly into a street parallel to the one they had started from and cut briskly through the business section. Nick followed him easily, picking his way politely through the pedestrian traffic and waiting patiently at stop lights. He stopped at a flower stall to buy himself a boutonniere and decline the offer of a shoeshine, and watched his man turning into the Avenida Independencia.

The man slowed his pace and dawdled on the sidewalk opposite Nick's hotel until something seemed to decide him to move on. Nick glanced across the street. There was nothing out of the way, so far as he could see, and the Police Chief's car hadn't yet arrived. He checked his watch. Twenty minutes to two. He hoped his man would go to cover soon.

He did.

His movement was so sudden that Nick almost missed it while concentrating on making his own movements seem appropriately casual. He was a roving diplomat, taking in the sights of the city while waiting for his touring car to . . .

The corner of his eye caught Green Face turning briskly into a doorway under a sign reading "Herbalist." Nick strolled slowly to within a few doors of the place and gazed entranced into an art store window. Five minutes was enough of that. The shop next door was a Beauty Parlour. He skipped it and spent some time looking into the window of an ultra-modern drug store. The shop next door was the herbalist's. His man had not come out. How like Africa, Nick thought, to put the drug store next to the herbalist's and let you take your choice. He ambled over to the next window, with a few minutes still to kill before meeting his car and with no intention of flushing out his quarry.

The window was a fascinating junkpile of suggestively shaped roots and small bottles filled with revolting fluids. An ancient elephant's foot served as a tray for an assortment of dried bones and tufts of hair, and a sunburned sign exhorted him to SHOP HERE FOR WONDER DRUGS AND MIRACLE CURES. It was dark inside the shop and the crammed window almost obscured the counter. But he could see enough to know that the man behind the crowded counter was old and wizened and that the man who faced the old one was the man he had been following.

He decided to go in and buy an amulet.

The door came open with a rusty jangle of bells. There was a swish and a slam at the rear of the shop, and as the door closed behind him he saw that he and the old man were alone in the store. He blinked dazedly as if to accustom himself to the gloom, but he saw every detail of the musty little shop and knew that there was a door behind a curtain that was still swaying. He could even hear the footsteps going up uncarpeted stairs.

"Help you, sir?" the proprietor crooned. "Souvenir? Love potion? Strength of elephant or heart of lion? Or do you wish to look around?"

"I'd love to look around," Nick said truthfully, "but right now I haven't got time. A good luck charm, that's all I need. Something to ward off evil."

"Ah! Many kinds of evil, many kinds of charms." The old man busied himself beneath the counter. "This one, against wicked men. This for illness. This, to bring success in business..."

"I'll take that," Nick said, noting that it was a relatively clean old coin while most of the other offerings were shapeless little bags or yellowed teeth, and also noting the brand new telephone that squatted so incongruously on the counter. He paid the man and slipped the charm around his neck while his eyes found the telephone wires that ran up one low wall and through the ceiling.

"I wonder if I might use your telephone," he said suddenly. "I see that I am late for an appointment." He put some of his change back on the counter and lifted the receiver without waiting for an answer. The old man sucked in his breath sharply.

"Oh, no! I am sorry, Senhor... M'sieu! No, I am afraid you cannot." He anxiously pulled the phone away from Nick and pushed down the bar. "It does not work very well—I am afraid it is out of order."

Nick raised his eyebrows. "It seemed to be working very well," he said coldly. "I distinctly heard another voice on the line."

"That is the trouble," the old man panted, making what Nick thought was a rather good recovery. "There always seem to be other voices on the line. There are telephones across the street at the hotel. I am sure you will find better service there."

"All right. I'll try." Nick irritably took back his change and walked out of the shop. The bells clanged discordantly behind him.

He looked across the street at his hotel. Its main entrance was almost directly opposite. Some of its windows were straight across from the small window above the "Herbalist" sign. Very convenient, he thought, wondering how long the herbalist had had his telephone—or phones. He also wondered how he had been fortunate enough to draw a room in the rear overlooking the quiet square.

It was still a few minutes before two and there was no car waiting for him in front of the hotel. It suddenly struck him that there were very few cars on the streets at all; perhaps it was something to do with the long lunch hours he'd heard about. Two cars were parked just beyond the loading zone of the hotel, both empty and another idled on a corner while its driver chatted with someone on the sidewalk. The atmosphere was so strangely quiet that it was somehow not peaceful at all.

Nick thought of the fragments of speech he had heard on the telephone. A deep voice had said in French: "... dangerous to wait." The second voice was a strange mixture of nasal whine and sibilance, and it had said plaintively: "But we must find out what..."

And a little old man who sold herbs and charms had abruptly cut him off. A little old man who was about as unlikely a candidate for high-powered international intrigue as Nick had ever seen.

Nick stepped off the curb and felt that familiar, crawling tingle at the back of his neck. He almost turned, but he made himself walk on into the street. There was no sense tipping off Green Face too soon—he'd find out much more by stringing him along. And, by the same token, Green Face had no reason—yet—to put a bullet in the back of Nick's head.

The roar of the motor slammed through Nick's ears and ripped his thoughts apart. The idling car no longer idled; it threw itself at Nick like an angry elephant but with much greater speed. Tyres screamed and a horn blared furiously and Nick threw himself forward to miss the monster by inches. He cartwheeled on to the sidewalk and drew himself up by a lightpole, reaching reflexively for Wilhelmina. A police whistle shrilled and something flew past his ear to slap into the wall behind him and roll back almost to his heels. Thoughts of grenades leapt into his mind but he saw instantaneously that it was a rough stone with a piece of paper wrapped around it. A motorcycle cop roared out of a side street and flung after the fleeing car. Wilhelmina stayed where she was.

Nick picked up his cane and the stone and peeled off the wrapping paper. The crudely scrawled message read: YANKEE MURDERER GO HOME!

Abe Jefferson's car was engaged for some time that afternoon before it was free to take Nick on the tour and so was the Chief of Police. When they did meet briefly, it was only to exchange rapid bursts of information and arrange an evening meeting. In the end it was Tad Fergus who acted as guide while Uru lashed the big car into breathtaking feats and Stonewall sat stolidly beside him with his tremendous right hand resting on his gun butt.

"Look, keep your car," Nick had protested vigorously. "Let somebody from the Embassy take me."

Jefferson's refusal was emphatic. "Mr. Fergus will show you around, since I cannot, but I insist that you take my car. It is bulletproof, whereas the Embassy cars are not. And Vice-President Adebe is using the only other safe car in the city. No, please do not argue. I have my hands full as it is."

Nick capitulated. "What news about the President?"

" 'As well as can be expected,' the doctors say. I personally do not know what that means. But I would say that somebody has leaked out the story, or at least part of it. I don't know who it could have been. But there is an undercurrent in the city that I do not like. You must be very careful."

At Nick's request Tad directed Uru to take them to all sites of shootings and explosions in the vicinity of Abimako. They drove along the seashore between the brilliance of the sea and the biting blue of the sky and then inland to the small mission stations on the outskirts of the city and the lovely, lazy suburbs where the Russian residents lived. The lanky, redheaded Tad filled in the background with vivid detail and a wealth of knowledge that warmed Nick to him, and crisply gave him capsule reports of eyewitness accounts and local reactions to the incidents. Nick stopped at damaged homes and shattered warehouses, picking his way thoughtfully among the ruins until he had seen enough to set a pattern in his mind. Then they drove back into the heart of town and stopped at the old fort that served both as the Presidential residence and the Government Offices to meet various officials and see the site where Julian Makombe had been shot.

Nick's only non-business question of the afternoon related to Miss Elizabeth Ashton.

"How is she?" Tad looked at him, surprised. "Why, fine. Busy at the office this afternoon. You'll see her later, at the Patricks."

So Liz hadn't told him what had happened that morning. Nick felt oddly pleased. "Who are the Patricks?"

"Oh, sorry, I forgot to tell you. They're friends of the Ambassador's. Dinner there tonight with Sendhor and Adebe and Rufus Makombe and several others. The Ambassador and his wife are staying with the Patricks; have been since the Embassy was bombed. Nice people."

They were nice people, Nick discovered that evening. So nice that they didn't even seem to think he was being undiplomatic when he wandered off into the garden with Liz during the pre-dinner cocktail hour.

"I'm surprised to see you looking so full of beans and vigour," said Nick approvingly. In the soft afternoon light, with the sun gleaming over her dark hair and her creamy, flawless skin, Liz looked more delectable than ever. Her wide, huge eyes looked directly into his with a frankness he seldom met in his profession. For the first time in years he wondered briefly if his own eyes revealed the counter-plotting and the murder that lay behind them. "How's the shoulder?"

"A little sensitive, that's all. Abe's doctor looked at it; it's fine. How was your day?" She dismissed the subject of her shoulder carelessly.

He told her what he thought she should know, and they talked with growing ease beneath the swaying leaves and brilliant wild trees that arched above their heads. As they talked he became increasingly aware of the warmth and vitality of the tall and generously proportioned girl beside him.

"We'd better get back to the others," she said at last. "I really wanted to talk to you alone for a minute to tell you about your invitation."

"Invitation?"

"Uh-huh." The small lines crinkled at the corners of her eyes. "We've regretted not putting you up in true ambassadorial splendour. And since this morning ... well, I had to mention to Ambassador Thurston that there was some little contretemps in your hotel room, and he was most upset. Oh, I just said that your room was searched, that's all. It's up to you to tell him whatever you think best. But he was very concerned, and after beating about the bush for about fifteen minutes he finally managed to suggest that I ask you to stay with me, since my Aunt Abigail is visiting and can be our chaperone. So naturally, I agreed. Don't worry, I have lots of room. A darling little house in N'domi—that's a suburb—about five minutes' walk from everything."

Nick raised his eyebrows at her. "That's a very tempting invitation," he said, turning its advantages over in his mind. "And very kind of you to let yourself get pushed into it. But are you sure Aunt Abigail won't mind?"

Liz smiled cheerfully. "Quite sure. She left last week—how could she mind?"

They laughed so much that Tad Fergus came to find out what the joke was. They fobbed him off with an ancient elephant story and went into formal dinner in the Patricks' enormous panelled dining room.

The Nyangese guests did their best to be cordial but it was clear that they were worried and distracted. Vice-President Adebe left early with his lovely chocolate-coloured wife and a harried looking Sendhor. Rufus Makombe, about to leave after ignoring Nick all evening, changed his mind suddenly on hearing a fragment of converstaion and made a point to draw Nick into a corner. In his clipped but lyrical language he apologized for his earlier coolness—"Inexcusable bad manners"—and begged indulgence. With the preliminaries over, he said: "So you are going to Dakar? I hope you have found some important lead to take you there. We need it; we desperately need it." His strong young face was taut and a tiny muscle twitched uncontrollably. "You do not realize—but of course you do. Have you found out something?"

Nick nodded slowly. "Not much. Just enough to make me want to look around outside the borders of this country."

Rufus nodded with satisfaction. "Ah! I also feel it is something bigger than this little country of Nyanga, If you have no hotel reservations, may I suggest the Hotel Senegal? It is not so lavish as the N'Gor, but it is much more convenient and I am well known there. I can arrange the booking, if you wish."

"That's very thoughtful of you, but please don't bother. Perhaps if I mention your name . . .?"

Rufus nodded vigorously. "Do that, and they will give you the hotel. I wonder if you are by any chance interested in some form of entertainment? Probably not anything too frivolous, but there is a place called the *Kilimanjaro* where there is magnificent entertainment in the true African style." His words hung questioningly in the air.

"If there's time, I'd be most interested," Nick answered. "What sort of place is it?"

"Not a club, not a club," Rufus shook his head emphatically. "I cannot quite describe it to you because there is nothing exactly like it in Europe or America. No liquor is served, only many kinds of wine. Also very strong African beer. No meals, but many interesting little sample dishes of regional specialities. There is a circular stage in the centre of the one big room, and there you will see such entertainment as you have never seen. The African High Life, you have heard of that? Yes, there is that. And the drums of the Congo, and the Chopi pianos. Also magnificent singing of the songs of our tribes and our cities. Nothing borrowed from other cultures. All our own!" The crest of his enthusiasm suddenly dropped him and the light went out of his eyes. He ended lamely, "Well, perhaps you will not like it. I only mention it in case you wish to experience something remarkable that you will never find in Washington."

The party broke up shortly afterwards.

Liz took Nick home with her in her own battered old car, which she handled with an assurance that pleased him. He noticed that she kept a wary eye on the rear-view mirror and the cross streets and was driving faster than was necessary on the quiet residential streets.

"Is it armoured?" he asked sardonically.

"Huh?" Liz kept her eyes on the road.

"Your car. The Chief's concerned about bullet-proofing me. Far more concerned than I am."

"Oh. No, of course it isn't. But he was the one who suggested that his big battlewagon might look a bit conspicuous sitting outside my place. With any luck, no one'll find out you're staying with me. The Ambassador's sworn to secrecy. Of course I told Abe Jefferson."

"Of course." He eyed her ample good looks with a slight feeling of resentment. She and Abe and the Ambassador were arranging him to death. Maybe one of these days he'd actually be allowed to make some decisions for himself.

She caught his eye. "Don't feel bad about us pushing you around," she said, with an extraordinary flash of intuition. "It's just that you're an important visitor who mustn't be bothered with trifles. Besides, we want to keep you safe. We like you—had you noticed?"

And she liked his answering smile.

"I've noticed a good many things that I like very much," he answered, "and you're one of them. And because of that, I'm not so sure it's a good idea for me to stay with you. I could be a danger to you."

"Guess who thought of that?" she said, manoeuvring

the wheel and darting the old car up a narrow side street. "We'll have plainclothes-police protection. We'll be able to come and go as we please. But no one else can. Is that all right with you?"

"Great. And my checkout from the hotel? My baggage? Have you arranged that, too?"

"Uh-huhm."

"Abe Jefferson?"

"Abe Jefferson. He will call—let's see—one hour and fifty minutes from now."

Liz turned briefly and flashed a grin at him. "You see, we have you all wrapped up."

Moments later she slid the serviceable car into her garage, murmured a greeting to a dark young man who slid out of the shadows then slid back again, and let Nick into her house. The latch clicked decisively behind them.

Her house was like her. Soft, sturdy carpeting and big lamps that gave off a comforting and mellow glow. Big, vivid pictures on the walls, modern, but not abstract. Splashes of wild flowers in bright ceramic vases, and huge chairs for sinking into. A vast, embracing sofa and a pile of gaily coloured cushions.

What happened was inevitable.

THE DIPLOMATIC TOUCH

THEY had a glass of wine, and he asked about her shoulder. She told him, showed him, and they kissed.

The shoulder was no bother at all, Neither were the soft folds of the evening dress that slid, unhindered, down the full length of her desirable form. Her breasts were like small mountains begging to be scaled, and the peaks were rose-shaped lollipops demanding to be tasted.

There was time; he took it, and she made it fly. It was all so natural and irresistible that he scarcely noticed how it had begun. One moment they were fully dressed and sipping wine and talking about men who carried knives to fling at unsuspecting Second Secretaries, and the next moment they were naked together and hardly talking at all.

She drew him close to her with one wonderfully supple arm and let the other play gently over his tanned, muscular body. He touched the marvellous full breasts and tasted them, and held her close to him for some time without moving just to feel the soft, firm length of her against him. She matched him perfectly. His hard muscles strained against her pliant strength and soon he was no longer lying quietly beside her but discovered her urgently. There was a perfume about her that was not Paris or New York or London but just Liz—a kind of clean freshness that reminded him of fresh-cut grass and freshwater mountain streams. And there was an exuberance about her that was not wanton but exhilarating. He buried his face in her hair while his arms encircled her body and said things that surprised him.

"I want to be with you in a haystack," he murmured, "with the hay in your hair all over you. I want to roll you over in it and make you laugh so you can't breathe, and love you till you lie back gasping. I want to take you on the beach, in the sand and under the water, and dry you myself and make love to you again. And I want you now . . . right now . . . I want you now."

Their mouths melted together and their bodies clung. Her warmth and gentleness enveloped him and he sank himself into the fulness of her body, excited by the wonderful size and shape of her and elated by her response to him.

By unspoken consent they prolonged each moment and lived it to the fullest, luxuriating in each lingering sensation and repeating it in half a dozen different, delicious ways.

She laughed once, in the middle of a voluptuous sigh.

"What is it?" he asked idly, fondling the luscious mound of her left breast and watching it come into flower.

"Just thinking of my position," she whispered. "Lady diplomat of rank. And yours. Special emissary, awesomely important . . ."

"I try to be special," he said modestly. "And as for your position, it is almost perfect."

What she could do with her magnificent body and all its large-scale wonders was a revelation and delight. She was absolute comfort and contentment, a refuge after a long journey, a refuge that offered its own thrills and surprises.

He went on thinking in terms of haystacks and beaches and soft grass while they clung together and moved in a perfect rocking rhythm that was tranquillity and excitement wrapped up in one. She was like some glorious slightly-larger-than-life statue suddenly and miraculously come to life. No; that was wrong. She had never been a statue, never been cold. Then she was mother earth, embracing him, doing these incredibly delicious things to him. Uh-uh. Liz was nibbling his ear and swivelling against him in a provocative way that suggested the favourite of the harem rather than a mother. And the things she breathed into his ear were not for children. Then she was a mountain that lay beneath a blanket of deceptively soft grass and pretended to be tranquil until the giant came to rouse her . . . He hadn't known he could be so fanciful. He was getting lightheaded with the wonder of her. Every move of hers was sudden pleasure laced with lingering magic; each touch of trailing fingertip and tightening of firm young muscle was a new excursion into a world of forbidden delights that suddenly were his.

The mountain *was* only pretending to be tranquil. It shivered and shook and changed colour and turned into a volcano.

Two beautifully muscled, finely tuned and energetic bodies merged and clashed and merged again. Mountains, statutes, beaches, soft grass all be damned. These were two people of more than ordinary proportions and bigger-than-everyday passions, making uninhibited and galvanic love on a giant-size sofa in a house belonging not exactly to a giantess but to a passionate witch with nothing small about her—neither her perfect body nor her capacity for love and laughter nor her enthusiasm for life. They joined together in a crescendo of emotion and physical sensation and stretched the moment of perfection for an incredibly long time. And then the earth moved and the room turned upside down.

At last they lay back, panting. Liz released a long, tremulous sigh. Nick's own body was trembling with the aftershock. He let the tremors roll away and then pulled her close to him again so that he could feel the heavenly breasts against his chest. They lay together with eyes half-closed, arms around each other, until their breathing became steady and the warm glow of release seemed to fill the room. And then they talked a little, just to get to know each other.

She sat up suddenly and said: "Abe Jefferson."

Nick sat up too. "You mean you checked this with him, too?"

"Silly." She grinned at him. "He'll be here soon. He wants to talk to you."

"Oh Christ, that's right." He started pulling on his clothes. Liz disappeared into the bathroom and came back in seconds wearing a long hostess gown that made her look dignified and desirable at the same time. Nick was busy with drinks, fixing something tall and cold and refreshing after the love and wine. His tie was slightly crooked and his thick hair, sometimes so slick, flopped down over one eye. His jacket straddled the back of a chair.

"Does Abe have the password?" he asked, handing her a drink. "We can't let just anybody in here, you know."

"Oh, yes." She sipped gratefully. "It's something I remember from when I was a little girl, and the boys used to say it: 'Button your lip, pull up your zip . . .' " She stopped suddenly and blushed. "I don't know what there is about you that makes me *say* things like that. But you'd better put your jacket on."

Nick slid into his jacket and regarded her with interest. "You must have been a depraved little girl. Under what circumstances did you hear this particular rhyme?"

"Never mind. Straighten your tie."

The doorbell gave off three short, sharp bursts of sound. Liz glanced swiftly into a pocket mirror and dabbed powder on her nose. Nick stood there laughing at her.

"Please," she said. "Your glasses. Your dignity. Your stuffed shirt. What have you done with them?"

He transformed himself for her, starting by slicking

back his hair and ending by assuming a pompous air.

"Only I don't think Abe Jefferson particularly expects it of me," he said as he completed the transformation. "But I'd better keep up appearances—you're absolutely right."

The doorbell rang again. Liz started towards it.

"I'll get it," said Nick. "You stay out of line of the door. Get over in the corner. And this time *do as I say*."

Liz stepped aside a little shamefully. Nick went to the door. "Who is it?" he called.

"Jefferson." It was Abe, unmistakably. "But be careful how you open the door. Don't make yourself a target."

Nick clicked the latch and drew the heavy door in towards him, stepping back with it and using it as a shield. He let one eye peer cautiously around the edge to seek the dimly lit figure of Abe Jefferson, standing expectently on the far side of the door frame.

"Get him, Sergeant," Jefferson said softly. There was a movement in the shrubbery behind him.

For one incredulous moment Nick thought the Chief of Police had ordered an attack on him. And the second moment almost proved it.

A sizzling bolt of lightning flashed into the room and lashed at the far wall before rebounding on to an overstuffed chair and then on to the carpeted floor. It lay there smoking and sizzling and giving off little tongues of flame.

"What the *hell*!" Liz cried out indignantly, and made a move towards the flaming object.

"Oh, for the luvva *Christ* do as I tell you and stay where you damn well are!" Nick roared back, even as he leapt with one arm outstretched to slam the door shut and the other reaching for the burning thing.

The flames flickered out as he touched it. It was a burnished assegai with a razor-sharp arrowhead of a tip, and it smelled of petrol. If it had hit anyone, it could have killed. And if it had landed on something instantly flammable, it would have made the most godawful of messes.

Wheels screamed on the rough pavement outside and someone hammered on the door.

"Come on, Carter, let me in." Abe Jefferson sounded plaintive. "I have a man going after him. Open up!"

Nick opened the door, still holding the wicked spear.

"You sure there aren't any more? I thought it was your calling card."

Abe Jefferson gave him a curdling look and closed the door behind him.

"It is *not* my calling card. Miss Ashton, I am so very sorry."

Liz came out of her corner with the fight gone out of her.

"Abe you look as though you haven't slept for weeks. Sit down and have a drink."

Jefferson sat down with a groan of exhaustion. "Thank you, but I do not drink on duty."

"You're not on duty in my house," Liz said decisively, and poured him a healthy dose of imported Bourbon on the rocks. Nick fingered the still-warm assegai and told himself that incidents not of his own making had gone far enough.

Jefferson gulped his drink gratefully and sighed.

"I see there was no message attached to that," he said. "But it was not aimed exclusively at you. Every American in town has had one of those tonight. Dick Webb of the Embassy caught one in the shoulder. The Patricks put out a fire in their living room. And Tad Fergus came home to find his bedroom smouldering. The others were like this—they fortunately did no damage. Some of them came with a message. The message said 'Yankee murderers go home.' It is obvious that this town is at fever pitch. This is misguided retaliation." He drained his glass and added, "At least, I hope it is misguided."

"It's misguided," Nick said quietly, "but I don't think it's retaliation. Like the bombing of the Embassy. Did you know that the same bombs were used in the bombing of the Russian Embassy and ours?"

Jefferson stared at him. "We do not have facilities for comparing that sort of evidence," he said stiffly. "That is not the report we had from Moscow."

"No, perhaps not. But that's the report *we* had from

Moscow and our own laboratories. What's happening is a calculated double-play. First put Americans in a bad light, then try to scare them off with this phoney retaliation stuff. But we don't scare off. And we don't fall easily for put-up jobs. I was hoping you don't either. In the light of all that's happened today... Oh, by the way, did Hakim get home safely?"

Abe Jefferson's strained face broke into a smile. "Yes, thank God; at least that one thing went right. He spoke most highly of you. We put a watch on that herbalist's shop, as you suggested. There are two little rooms upstairs and the old man lives in one of them, or so they tell us at the Beauty Shop. The crone, who runs it, who calls herself Héléne knows practically everything that goes on in her neighbourhood. She says that a man named Laszlo, whom she describes as being turtle-faced and snaky, has been occupying the other room on and off for the last six months. Sometimes she doesn't see him for weeks, and then he comes and stays for several days. He returned yesterday, after an absence of a week or so, and then he must have gone out during the night since he came back *twice* again today—first quite early, soon after she opened, and then again between one-thirty and two. She also saw you, and described you as being very handsome and distinguished but rather high-nosed. 'Thinks he's bloody important,' is what she said." He grinned. His tiredness seemed to have peeled off him and his humourous eyes were alert.

"Very perceptive old bag," Nick observed without rancor. "And since then?"

"Laszlo went out once, to eat. For the rest he seems to have been clinging to that room. As you know we have no right or reason to search it or question him. Nor to tap the old man's telephone, which we find has an extension upstairs. As for the various eavesdropping devices in your room, we found their source in the room above yours. Though we were ready to catch any hasty departures after we ripped the wires out, nobody left. And nobody was there. There was a tripping device to work a tape recorder when you used your telephone, and another slow-running recorder listening into your room. Obviously, whoever placed them there need only return at a convenient time to play back the tapes. So naturally we staked out the room and the corridors with subtly concealed individuals, and waited. Oh, we were *most* clever." His tone dripped self-contempt. "The only person who came near the room was the electrician with a neat little tale of checking a short in the landing wires. He went about his business and left. It was not until hours later, when Stonewall came back to check on his men, that we realised an electrician was the very man for the job. By that time he had vanished. We have a description, but we have lost him completely."

"Was anyone registered for that room? Were any outgoing calls made from it?"

Jefferson looked at Nick with a certain respect. "I'm afraid that is something that took us some time to think of, too. No, the room was supposed to be empty. This is not a busy time of year for the Hotel Independence—even though that is where everybody who is anybody at all stays when they come to Abimako. No calls have been made from it since it was last officially occupied. But the desk clerk—also something of a gossip, like the impossible Hélène—saw the hotel's electrician use the public phone booth in the lobby twice this morning. The first time was apparently while we were at the hospital. He is very vague about the second time; around lunchtime, he thinks."

"So the chances are he was reporting to someone," said Nick.

Liz glided about quietly, refilling the glasses and flashing approving looks alternately at Nick and Jefferson.

"It's not that I want to drag myself into your exclusively male conversation," she said at last, "but might not our knifer-with-the-embarrassed-behind be able to shed some light on that? His orders surely must have come from whom ever the electrician reported to."

The Chief's look was bitter. "He is as innocent as the day is long. He just happened to be passing by, broke and hungry, and he nipped in to look for money. We can't shake him. Not yet, that is. We're trying. Same with the characters we caught in the car that tried to run you down,

Carter. They wanted to scare you off because they hate Americans, they said. And that's all we've managed to get out of them."

"How about the fellow with the cloak? The one I put to sleep?"

"Picked him up to keep him from reporting back. He's cooling off until he talks, but he might as well have bitten his tongue out . . ."

It was the same story over and over again. The dead couldn't talk and the live ones wouldn't. The pattern was repeated when Stonewall arrived with Nick's baggage and a report on the throwers of the flaming spears.

"Found one, killed one," he reported glumly. "The live one is as silent as the dead. Glassy-eyed with hemp when we picked him up and now does nothing but shiver and moan."

The last cheerful bulletin of the evening was that the President was hovering on the brink of death and that the news of his condition would have to be made public if there was no improvement within the next two hours or so.

Abe Jefferson stumbled off to bed and said he'd call as soon as he heard anything new. Nick showered, kissed Liz very tenderly and lay beside her until she drifted into sleep. Then he rose silently and put on his working clothes.

It took time to ease himself out of a rear window silently enough to avoid Abe's watchers. Even then he scrunched on the gravel when he thought he was clear and had to wait for nearly half an hour in the shadows before he was sure of himself. After that it was easy going under the intensely black African sky, and he reached the corner of the Avenida Independencia without encountering anyone.

The Avenue itself was more of a challenge. He waited on his corner until he could distinguish the watchdogs in the gloom, and he began to wish that Abe hadn't been so thorough. There were at least three men watching the front of the herbalist's shop from various angles. The lane at the back was a different proposition. It was open at one end only, and there was a solitary watcher across from it, pacing back and forth like a leopard in a cage. Abe must have been running short of qualified men; the fellow was not a clever watcher. He was obvious, and he was bored. He was so obvious that Nick was not the first one to get past him.

Nick flitted silently into the lane and clung like a slowly moving shadow to the rear walls of the low buildings fronting on the Avenue. Surely, he thought, there should have been another watcher in the lane.

He was right. There had been. He lay at the far end of the lane with his face in a dark, sticky pool, the back of his head dented hideously and matted with drying blood. Nick paused long enough to be sure that nothing could be done for him and to draw on the special fingerprintless, skin-thin gloves made for him by AXE's Editing Department.

He counted back doors until he knew he was behind the herbalist's shop. There were no lights showing from within, and the lock gave without a struggle against Nick's Lockpickers' Helper. His pencil beam swept the shop and found it empty of everything but the junk he'd noticed earlier. He retraced his steps to the back stairway and started climbing stealthily, one hand lightly on the rail and the other holding the lethal Wilhelmina. A sagging stairboard complained like a startled cat and he froze for moments, waiting. Nothing stirred.

There were two doors on the tiny landing both closed but neither of them locked. He fingered one open, very quietly, and sidled in. Still there was no sound. His small flashlight flicked on and probed around a tiny, filthy room with shuttered windows, an unmade bed and several rickety sticks of furniture, including a battered old armchair. The beam caught the chair and held it.

The room's occupant sat slumped in the chair at a curiously awkward angle. The clothes it wore were those of an upperclass workman, a foreman of some kind or possibly an electrician. The shirtfront was dreadfully stained. Nick catfooted over and raised the head.

It grinned horribly at him. The grin was under the chin, and it reached from ear to ear in hideous welcome. Nick let the head fall on to the bloodstained chest and swiftly scanned the rest of the room. Empty food cans and a grimy spoon in the closet. Thick dust under the bed. Nothing in the open bureau drawers but little scraps of trash.

He doused the light and crept quietly across the tiny landing to the other room. It was very much the same as the first one, except that it was cleaner and the bed was occupied.

His flashlight beam shone down on the dark face against the pillow. Two eyes stared back at him. Two old, stone-cold dead eyes.

PIERRE GETS THE CREEPS

The old herbalist had not been dead for very long. About as long as the plainclothesman in the lane, maybe, but not as long as the man with the permanent grin. And he had not died easily.

His legs were halfway out of the bed and the bedclothes were thrown back as if he had been getting up when someone had stopped him with two downward slashes of a knife and then left him for dead.

That was their mistake. The old man had bled copiously, and the still-wet blood made a pattern on the pathetic old nightshirt that showed that he had struggled to an awkward half-lying, half-sitting position and twisted to one side. Nick's light slid from his body to the small table at the bedside. Its single drawer was open and revealed a typical old man's collection of pills and cures obtained from the nearby modern drug store and some loose papers. Most of them were bills and receipts and some were blank notesheets. A couple of them had fluttered down to the floor. Nick turned the light on them and saw that they were also blank. Near them, almost under the bed, lay a chewed, blunt stub of pencil.

The light flickered back across the bed and the agonized face stared up at Nick accusingly. After trying to sit up the old man had fallen back on the bed and his scrawny arms lay limply by his sides. But the right hand was loosely open and the left was clenched into a fist. An edge of paper protruded from the gnarled black hand. Nick forced back the clutching fingers and withdrew it.

It was a pitiful attempt at a message. Nick stared at it for moments before he managed to decipher the painfully formed words. There werd only two of them, and they seemed to be: *Eyes Dakar.*

Eyes ... Dakar. He burned the words into his mind while he stuffed the paper into his pocket and made a lightning inspection of the room. There was nothing there but an old man's carelessly kept clothes and few personal things. The single window looked down on the dark, back lane. Nothing stirred.

Nick left the one dead man and went back across the tiny landing to the other. He had left no messages, but Nick found a card identifying him as Alfred Gore, Electrician, Hotel Independence. The room smelled of blood, alcohol, and something else that Nick could not identify. An empty glass beside Gore's chair reeked of the local whisky, and so did the man's horribly stained shirtfront. Laszlo of the Green Face and bulging eyes had evidently entertained him well before saying goodbye. There was no sign of the bottle or anything else ... Bulging eyes. Eyes, Dakar. 'Eyes' had gone to Dakar?

And had covered his tracks behind him. Covered them with blood.

He had also taken with him anything that could possibly have been of any value to Nick, barring the scrawled note he had not known about. And of course the telephone extension that had been so handy for relaying information received from the hotel Independence.

Maybe there was something of interest in the shop.

The watchers on the Avenida Independencia were still at their posts, blobs of thick darkness in the thinner darkness. Nick left them at their fruitless vigil and quickly made his way downstairs. He double-checked the backdoor latch to make sure that no one could steal in while he was in the front room, and then opened the door to the shop.

Something small and somehow rather horrible scrunched beneath his feet as he drew back the curtain and stepped into the musty little room. Beetle or roach, he thought, without dwelling on it, and moved silently towards the dim light at the front of the shop so that he could both use its faint glow behind him to look around and also shield his flashlight beam with his own body. Something scuttled across his feet as he reached the front door. Suddenly he was conscious of other sounds in the room—slithering, scurrying, fluttering sounds—as his passage through the room awakened something and annoyed it. Like the something that had scuttled softly across his feet.

The pencil beam of his flashlight swung low around the room, picking at the dusty shelves and searching for the eerie presence. He was the only human being in the room unless . . .

His light jabbed at the floor. Something made one of those infinitesimal little movements and stopped a yard away from him. The probing flashlight sought and found it. The thing looked back at him. It had a reddish brown body slightly larger than a silver dollar, and eight long, reddish furry legs. A slight chill touched Nick's spine. He saw a menace in miniature, a creature called "Red Devil" by the bush natives because its vicious spider's bite stabbed like a pitchfork, burned like the flames of hell, paralysed and killed:

It moved thoughtfully towards him, eyes glinting balefully in the pencil lightbeam.

Nick's first thought was to crush it underfoot. Then he remembered the incredible speed with which these horrors could move when aroused, and how Hank Todd had died, writhing, after he had tried to step on one in the Uganda bush. It also occurred to him, in that same instant, that there were other things slithering around the room.

Jump over it and run like hell? Can't get out of the front door—curse those useless watchers of Abe's. And God knows what other lurking things were waiting to sink their fangs into him while he fumbled with the curtained back door.

The creature stopped and looked at him. A soft hissing sound came from the rear of the room. Nick played the beam of the flashlight quickly over the floor, praying that

Red Devil wouldn't take a flying leap at him in the darkness.

His first thought was one of amazement that he had managed to cross the room without stepping on anything more than a beetle. But it was probably his footsteps that had snapped them all horrifyingly to attention.

A second red devil was emerging from behind the counter, followed by a lizard-like creature Nick had never seen before. Red devil number two scuttled under the rear door curtain and stayed there, an armed guard covering the only possible exit. The floor between it and the first spider seemed to be twitching with strange life—spiders, beetles, lizards, scorpions of enormous size, and snakes. Jesus Christ, what snakes! Two—no, three, four—tiny, squirming, spitting bundles of death. Gaboon vipers, was it? The hell with the name. They were vipers, and they were murder.

A bat swooshed above his head. Nick started very slightly, and the devil near his feet zigzagged closer to him. The whole floor rippled and shuddered. It seemed to be converging on him like one vast, wallowing monster.

The flashlight, in its travels round the room, had found the shelves and counter and the tiny beasts and one straight-backed grimy chair that must have been used by clients waiting for some weird prescription of dead herbs and living venom. It might yet be Nick's salvation.

He moved his feet cautiously and let the thin-beamed light play over the floor. The floor between him and the curtained door was writhing and hissing with strange life. He had time to curse himself for reacting too slowly to the slithering, shuffling sound—yet it was only seconds since he had come into the room. Then the creatures closest to his feet—the red spider, and a vicious little fork of lightning that he knew to be a viper—were moving in with terrible swiftness. He heard the hiss, and then he jumped.

The ancient chair teetered, fell back against the nearby wall, and straightened, creaking ominously. Even before it stopped its wild staggerings Nick had found his balance and was reaching into his pocket for the only tool that could possibly help him. As he found its reassuring smooth, round shape he thought with grim humour of his own predicament. Ridiculous, he told himself, as he clamped the light between his teeth and his strong fingers twisted the small shape of Pierre. Like a woman scared of mice, leaping on the nearest chair.

But the things that shuffled and hissed around the chair legs were more monster than mice, and some of them could climb. Red devil number-something was already reconnoitering the left front leg and showing every sign of getting ready to climb it.

Nick held his breath and gave Pierre one final twist and tossed him lightly into the centre of the writhing room.

The deadly gas pellet waited his usual thirty seconds before going silently to work. Pierre held a small but highly concentrated substance that sucked the air and gave back high-powered poison; Nick had seen strong men die of Pierre in seconds after the preliminary half-minute. But he had no experience with Pierre's effects on animals, insects and snakes.

While he waited, lungs full of musty air and his mind on creeping things and "Eyes... Dakar" he swung the flashlight beam slowly around the room and wondered how he'd let himself get caught. From his new height he could see the open cages and the empty tanks behind the herbalist's counter. Green-Face-Frog-Eyes must have had himself a nasty little ball after leaving for Dakar and killing a policeman on his way out. But why hadn't *he*, super-sleuth Nick Carter, been aware of these skittering, scuffling things before? He swore at himself as he asked the question, and realized at once that he had only looked for human occupants before going on his way up stairs. And Eyes must have left long enough before so that the creatures would have quieted down. Or shortly enough before so that they were not yet free...?

The flash beam licked the floor beneath his feet. A viper spat back at him. Its tiny body twitched as though readying itself to jump, and the vicious spitting mouth opened and closed against the thickening air.

A red devil appeared suddenly on the wooden seat beneath Nick's feet and tacked dazedly toward him. This time there was nothing to do but try to smash the creature. Nick raised his left foot and let death slither beneath it. The red devil sidled swiftly toward the standing right foot and Nick brought his free leg down in a lightning movement that would have befuddled any quick-thinking man. But the red spider was not a man. Some instinct made it dart free of the descending foot and scrabble up the outside of the right trouser leg. Nick's foot came down uselessly on the wooden seat and the thing clung to the fabric of his pants. He swung his leg suddenly and violently as if he were kicking off a football game, and still the thing clung to his right trouser leg. Nick brought his leg far back, past the side of the chair, so that the thing was clinging to cloth separated from Nick's vulnerable flesh by an inch of space. He felt it scuttle up to his knee, where the cloth was tighter and only its thickness separated him from death.

If he tried to strike it off, it would bite with deadly savageness. Wilhelmina would blow his knee to bits. Hugo could miss. The creaping bastard was still horribly alive and accurately swift. It was a wonder that it hadn't bitten yet. Feeling Pierre quite badly now, most likely. Any second now it could fall off and die.

It didn't. It tickled his knee and slithered up his thigh. Nick felt cold sweat breaking out on his forehead. He held the lower part of his body still and relaxed, as his Yoga training had taught him, and reached slowly and carefully into his jacket pocket for the only other weapon he had.

He drew it out silently and brought it up against the slight but awful weight that settled on his upper leg. His left thumb flickered urgently against the tiny, corrugated wheel and the harsh flame of his cigarette lighter bit into his thigh. But first it bit the red-brown killer that clung to him like a demon lover, and the thing jerked hideously as the glossy back and furry legs caught fire. The killing flame showed the shrivelling, convulsively kicking obscenity turning black, red sparks glinting at the base of its short hairs. It dropped on to the floor, a charred ball with eight bare, glowing legs. Its light went out.

Nick brushed out the small fire on his pants leg and willed himself not to feel the burning pain nor to breathe the acrid air. He stroked the flashlight beam across the floor. Ten little, nine little, eight little spider devils, seven little, six little, five little killer vipers, four little, three little, two little scorpions, one little green lizard dead. They drooped like dying leaves in the beam of his flashlight. At last the scuttling, fluttering, slithering noises stopped.

He waited another twenty seconds or so before stepping down from his perch into the sea of dead and crumpled things. Someone was walking slowly along the street outside. The footsteps stopped as he listened. Stopped and came back and stopped again just outside the window. He could see the dimness of the room thickening slightly as the figure blocked out most of the little light that filtered through the junkpile window from the street. It was one of Abe's men, and he had his nose almost pressed against the pane. Looking for a flickering light, no doubt thought Nick. Well, he isn't going to see it.

Nick bent into a low crouch and crept across the squishing floor beneath the level of the window. When he had cleared it and reached the shallow side of the room beyond the front door he straightened up and sidled to the back of the room, keeping one eye on the window and trying not to notice the repulsive sounds that came from underneath his feet. No one outside could possibly have heard them, but to him they sounded like bodies splattering on a sidewalk below the thirty-seventh floor.

He paused at the curtained door and watched Abe's man turn and walk on. By this time Nick's lungs were beginning to feel like over extended balloons and his ears were hearing the singing of a distant surf. He'd have to get outside—or to an open window—in a hurry. He chose the latter as he pushed aside the curtain and opened the inner door; there was no knowing what he might meet in the lane.

The stairboard creaked as usual as he raced up to the landing and threw himself into the old man's room. The dead eyes seemed to watch him with acute dislike and disapproval. Nick dropped to his knees at the partly open window and sucked in the cool night air. When his breathing became normal he raised the window as far as it would go, and then crossed into the other room to open the shutters and the shutter-type windows. To anyone watching it would seem a normal enough thing for a man to do in the middle of the night if he woke up in a stuffy room. A fresh draught swished across the upstairs landing. He wished he could open the back door to be sure that Pierre's lethal fumes would have dispersed by the time Abe's men decided to investigate the place, but that was much too chancy. Given the slightest break, Pierre would have enough time to leave quietly by the windows. He himself would probably have to do the same, and do it now.

Two of Abe's watchmen on the Avenida Independencia were standing together and conferring. Then one walked away and joined the third for another brief conference. Nick wondered if the men at the back were supposed to do the same. They must surely have periodic checks with each other.

The poor bloodsoaked bastard in the alley. First sight of him and they'd come come crashing into the house. He'd have to stall them somehow, even if only for minutes.

Nick filled his lungs with air and ran down into the mustiness of the lower floor. He unlatched the back door carefully and looked out through a narrow crack before stepping outside. The night was silent. His eyes and his senses told him that he was the only living thing in the lane. Then he pulled the door wide open.

Abe's backdoor-man was lying where Nick had found him. His blood was drying rapidly now in the rising breeze. The second of the rearguard watchers was out of sight, but Nick could hear two sets of quiet footsteps meet and stop. That made it seem that watcher number one checked with watcher number two; number two turned to number three; number three walked to number four; number four would look for number five and wouldn't find him; number four would whistle to number three and together they'd find Carter with three bodies and a mouthful of explanations. That kind of predicament would be embarrassing for the special representative of a government already deep in dutch with the Nyangese and their Russian friends. Nick's eyes skimmed the rooftops while he hoisted the unwieldly body. Maybe. Yes, he could make it if he had to. And he would almost certainly have to—it wasn't likely he could get past two living men alert to danger.

He hauled the cumbersome shape down the lane and through the open doorway, setting it down gently just inside the door. As he closed the door he heard the footsteps start again. This time there was only one pair of them, and they were coming closer. Holding his breath against the lingering death-fumes of Pierre, Nick locked the door hastily and took the stairs in several light, loping bounds. From a vantage point in the old man's room, near the window but hidden from outside, he looked down into the lane and saw Abe's man saunter towards the back door and past it. In seconds he was out of sight, his soft footfalls fading, stopping, and then getting louder again. He paused somewhere near the window and Nick could hear him give a low whistle. Again he started to walk, this time hesitantly as though he were peering into the shadows. If he peered into the right shadow, he'd be sure to see the blood.

But he walked back past the door and repeated the low whistle. Nick risked a quick look to see him reach the end of the lane and just stand there, staring around like a lost sheep. Without waiting for him to come to his senses Nick pulled himself on to the high windowsill and chinned himself swiftly up to the outer lintel. From there it was only a foot or so to the roof, which looked flat from below and was probably—he hoped—cement-finished or asphalted. He propelled himself upward with his feet pushing against the window frame and his arms reaching from lintel to edge of roof. In a moment he was grasping the edge and hauling himself up on to it. It *was* asphalted. A herd of elephants could walk across it and not be heard. He crouched low on it and looked down over the edge. The lane was empty for a moment, but as he watched a second man joined Abe's inept alley-watcher and the two of them pussyfooted warily into the lane with the exaggerated care of men walking on dinosaur eggs. Nick left them to their gruesome search and took off from his roof to the one next door at a silent running crouch. From there he could see that one of Abe's watchers was still at the front but the second was moving around to take the place of the one who had joined the fourth in search of their buddy. And a useless bloody lot they were, too, Nick thought disgustedly.

But they probably weren't trained for this sort of thing. Abimako's crimes, until recent months, had never been much more than simple thefts and occasional brawls. Besides that, all of Abe's best men were busy hunting for bomb-throwers and assassins.

His progress across the roof was as silent and unseen as a sleek black cat setting out at night across the tiles. He lowered himself just as quietly at the end of the block and crossed the street out of sight of the police-watcher on the Avenue. After that he made good time back to Liz's house, again approaching it slowly, cautiously.

He hoped Liz was still asleep.

Still as stealthy as a black cat, he let himself in through the window.

Liz was not in bed.

He found her in the living room sipping a cold beer and glancing at a magazine.

"You've been gone for simply hours," she said. "I woke up, I was thirsty, and I missed you. Have a bottle. You look thirsty, too."

Wordlessly, he took a beer bottle and flicked off the cap.

"What in the world have you been doing," Liz asked, managing to sound not so much nosy as politely interested, to get a hole burned in your pants?"

"Getting ready for Dakar," he said. "Cheers."

THE SILENT VISITOR

The Hotel Senegal in Dakar was all that Rufus Makombe had said it was, and more. So much more that as soon as Nick got to his room, after his swift morning flight from Abimako, he began to wonder if they weren't overdoing things a little. He also thought over the short list of people who had known he would be staying at the Senegal, and wondered if he shouldn't have obeyed his initial impulse to check in at the Majestic under one of his many imaginative pseudonyms.

He was thinking all these things in a series of simultaneous flashes as the bellhop, carrying his one bag, locked the door behind him, dropped the bag, and said almost as musically as Stonewall: "Put your hands up, white Yankee, and do not make a sound. You will die instantly if you call out."

Nick turned slowly with his hands half-raised and saw the muscular dark figure and the long-nosed gun with its cumbersome silencer. Cumbersome or not, it was a type he knew would stifle harsh reports sufficiently to let them pass unnoticed in this busy, chrome-plated palace on Dakar's noisiest street.

"You fool!" Nick hissed. "You treacherous blind fool!" His arms dropped to his sides. "Don't you even know who you're working for?" The gun faltered almost imperceptibly and Nick pressed his flickering advantage. "Tell me the words that were agreed upon or you will die like the creeping rat you are." The liquid eyes clouded with puzzlement but the gun steadied and pointed inexorably at Nick.

"There are no words..." the big man began. Nick cut him off with an exclamation that spat across the room.

"No words! You ignorant ape! Is that how much you know about our operations here? Pah! Put that foolish gun away at once or you will suffer for your idiocy. The Cause will not put up with such bunglers as you. Didn't you understand your orders, pig?"

The gun dropped hesitantly and Nick leapt. His sinewy hands caught hold and twisted agonizingly. The gun came free in his right hand and he slammed it lightly against the big man's temple. The fellow staggered and fell back. Nick drew back his leg and slammed his weighted heel against one flailing limb. It caught the shin where he'd intended and the big bellhop screamed and dropped.

"Now," said Carter menacingly. "Perhaps you will understand that you do not trifle with your superiors. Stop your whining and tell me instantly who caused you to make this unthinkable blunder. Weren't you told that the white Yankee made arrangements to check into the Majestic? And that I have come from headquarters to find out where he goes and who he sees? Sit up and talk to me as you have been taught. As I *hope* you have been taught."

The big man groaned and pulled himself painfully to a sitting position.

"I thought—they told me—who are you?" he stammered.

"*I* ask, you answer!" Nick snapped at him. "What were your orders, and who gave them to you, that you did not know my true identity?"

"Laszlo, Laszlo!" the man said earnestly. "He said the American Carter might come here and I was to..." He stumbled over his words and his eyes wandered over Nick's shoulder and pulled themselves away with visible effort. Nick twisted a swift look behind him and jumped simultaneously.

The flying figure that burst from the bathroom doorway missed Nick by inches and crashed into the big bellhop. Two big, muscular bodies sprawled on the floor and the first one cursed obscenely. The second extricated himself with a leaping turn and faced Nick in a crouch with his weird weapon raised. Nick flicked himself out of reach and pointed the bellhop's gun.

"Get back!" he ordered. "Get your hands up or I'll shoot."

The man lunged at him. Nick cursed softly and aimed for the bunched shoulder that was one great weapon in itself, starting from the straining neck and extending to the pointed tip of the weapon in the massive hand.

The gun clicked uselessly.

Nick cursed again and flung it viciously across the room as he wheeled sideways and let the man come at him. His body bent slightly forward, his steel-and-whipcord arms lashed out to push and pull in a series of swift moves so smoothly co-ordinated that they seemed like one. The wooden striking blade of the flat club—used like the hard edge of the hand in Karate—soared forward and down. Nick let it come toward him, then he pivoted and grasped the bulging arm that held the club and swung it downward like a pump handle. The left arm and foot flailed wildly in the air. Nick completed the twist and the man somersaulted floorward like a wheel ripped from its axle and rolling crazily. The man made a sound like a watermelon splitting open. Nick scooped up the sword-shaped club and tossed it after the gun. In this kind of fight he preferred to use his hands and feet. He kicked viciously at the groin. The man gave a groan like a mighty belch and jerked convulsively, drawing up his legs and clutching himself like a caterpillar curling itself into an aching ball.

Nick saw the movement near the bedroom door from the corner of his eye. His first assailant was raising himself painfully to one knee and pulling a knife from inside the jacket of his loose uniform. Nick watched the arm go back and start forward before he moved, and then he moved like greased lightning. The knife hissed past his ear and buried its thin blade in the hard wood of the closet door. Nick leapt up from his low crouch and flicked the knife straight out of the wood and snapped it back at its owner in one smooth motion. It caught the killer bellhop as he scrabbled painfully towards the door just as he reached upward for the doorknob. His upraised chin had made his thick neck an easy irresistible target. He gargled horribly and fell to the floor clutching his throat and hiccuping.

The second man was slowly uncoiling at Nick's feet. Nick, avoiding the man's outstretched, grasping hands. slid Hugo out of his slender sheath.

Hugo was a deceptively small Italian stiletto that concealed its deadly ice-pick blade in a thin bone handle until released by the flick of a finger on a tiny switch. Then Hugo would spring into fighting position, and fighting for Hugo was killing. Unless, of course, Hugo succeeded by gentle persuasion instead of dealing instant death.

Nick flicked the small trigger and Hugo darted out of hiding like a snake flashing out its tongue.

"Now sit up with your hands behind your back. Come on! Move!"

The man sat up slowly, making little grunting noises

and seeking a weapon with his eyes. When he saw the gun and his swordlike club at the far end of the room well out of his reach, he lost interest in them and stared hopefully at Nick's feet, his shoulders bunching reflexively as if his arms were itching to get at his captor.

Nick's grey eyes were cold, cruel steel as they gazed down at the captive.

"Now you're going to tell me where you get your orders," he said quietly in French. "You're not leaving here until you do. Understand?"

The dark head nodded, but there was a contemptuous smile on the fleshy lips.

"I don't think you do," Nick said. He strode to the bedroom door and locked it, keeping his eyes on the silent, cross-legged figure. "No one will be let in or out of this room until I have finished with you. And I will not finish with you until you have told me what I want to know." He moved back to his victim and looked down at him, thoughtfully fingering Hugo's tapering point. "It may hurt." He waited. The man said nothing. "Who sent you?" Nick said sharply. "Start with that and start now. Or *I'll* start."

The man shook his head emphatically.

"All right, start talking."

The man shook his head again. The muscles in Nick's face tightened. Killmaster or not, he didn't like what he was going to do.

"Then get up and turn your face to the wall." Nick's voice was ice and his mouth closed in a cruel, determined line.

The man looked back at Nick and got slowly to his feet, a big bullock of a fellow with deep, angular tattoo marks on his cheeks.

"Either turn around or talk," Nick lashed at him.

The man opened his mouth but neither turned around nor talked. Instead he leaned slightly forward and put his head back, pointing into his mouth like a kid bragging about a newly extracted tooth.

What was missing was not a tooth. It was his tongue.

Nick's eyes widened involuntarily as he stared.

The incomplete mouth closed and the tattooed face

took on an expression that was half-fearful, half-contemptuous.

"Who did that—the people you work for?" the question at least drew some reaction.

The head wagged vigorously from side to side.

"Who, then?" The tongue had been cut out many years before; perhaps his own people had done it. "Your tribesmen?" A negative shake of the head. "Rival? Witch-doctor?" Two more decisive shakes. "White man?" An emphatic, multiple nod, and a baring of the teeth. "Portuguese?" Again a nod. "French?" Another nod. "Belgian?" Nod. Nick raised a mental eyebrow, though his face was stony. What was this—a variation on the all-white-men-are-the-same theme? "American?" Emphatic nod. "Russian?" A half-nod that stopped in the middle. "Chinese?" A shaking, nodding, rolling motion accompanied by confusion of the eyes and a troubled frown. "English?" A nod that finished with a chin on the chest and downcast eyes. The man without a tongue knew he had goofed. "Recently?" No reaction. "Long ago?" No reaction.

Nick surveyed his victim without satisfaction. He and Hugo could probably extort something out of this man before the day was out. A jab here, a nod there, a pinprick now and a headshake then, and some kind of answer would eventually emerge. But would it be worth the time it would take? Doubtful. And there was no guarantee that he was going to be left undisturbed for as long as he needed.

"Put those hands behind your back and hold them there," he ordered. "That's better." Nick studied him. The man wore his European-style suit without ease, as though he were uncomfortable in it. And he wore his ill-fitting shoes as though they were instruments of torture. He was not an unusual type for an African city. Nevertheless...

"You can write, can't you?" Hugo wagged threateningly.

The man shook his head triumphantly. Hugo darted at his face with vicious speed and bit lightly into the fleshy part of his left cheek. He gasped and took an involuntary step back.

"*You can write, can't you.*" Hugo nipped hungrily at

the other cheek and withdrew with incredible speed.

The head shook violently. Surprise and pain replaced the scorn on the man's face and little mewling sounds came from his throat.

"Show me your hands. *Slowly*. Bring them from behind your back. One side first, then turn them over."

The hands reached slowly and—it seemed—supplicatingly towards Nick.

They were the scarred and calloused hands of a man who worked in the soil and on the carpenter's bench and maybe with bricks. None of the callouses had anything to do with holding a pencil or pushing a pen. Nick sighed silently to himself. It was not conclusive, but the man was probably telling the truth.

"All right, then. There's only one way you can answer me and you're going to do it. Remember, I'm armed with more than a knife. And I'm not alone, as you seem to think."

Blood trickled down the dark face from the two small perforations and two wary eyes watched Nick uncertainly.

"You're going to take me to the people who sent you here," Nick said conversationally. "And if you do it without trying to tip me to them you may even live through the meeting. Or you may not. Let's go. But first of all you can pick up that buddy of yours and put him in the closet. Hurry, friend. I haven't got all day."

Hugo sliced the air, waggling impatiently.

The man stayed where he was. He was cringing now and shaking his head without the slightest trace of arrogance or scorn, and pitiful gurgling noises came from his throat.

"Get moving." Nick's voice was as cold as Hugo's steel; and Hugo spoke as he did. The lightning blade slashed down one large, fleshy ear and slid gracefully off the bottom of the chin.

Nick's victim growled and backed away, shaking his head like a lion in pain. He seemed to be trying desperately to form words.

"What is it?" asked Nick. "Do you want someone to talk for you?"

The head swung wildly and the thick lips drew back to

show the teeth and gums.

"Then move!" Nick rapped.

The fellow moved with the speed of desperation and struck with the blind strength of terror. His arms tore at Nick's knife hand and the sounds he made were those of an animal fighting for its life. Nick let his grasp tighten, then pivoted on the balls of his feet and flipped the man over his shoulder to the floor.

"Get up!" he grated. "You've got one last chance to do as I tell you or you're through."

The man squirmed to his feet and stood there panting. Then he leapt again, grasping for the knife and grappling like a madman. Nick raised his knee sharply and brought it up into the dumb man's crotch. His visitor made an awful gasping sound but went on clawing at Nick. One tremendous arm tried to lever the knife arm down while the other went for Nick's face.

Nick threw him off once more.

"You fool!" he said, almost pleadingly. "Take me where I want to go—or I'll kill you."

The man drew himself into a crouch and leapt. Hugo met him in the air and plunged into his heart.

The body was still fighting for a life already lost when Nick pulled the twitching arms away from him and let the dead weight fall to the floor.

Nick moved swiftly then, thinking bitterly to himself of the hazards of hotel living and how he always managed to get his room cluttered up with dead or dying or escaping visitors. He dragged the stilled, speechless man into the bathroom. He had the bellhop halfway across the floor when his door vibrated with a heavy knock. He dumped the man on to his companion in the bathroom and ripped off his own jacket and tie. When he reached his bedroom door he picked up his bag, tossed it on the bed and opened it. He tore off his shirt and tossed it on to the nearest chair. His feet moved smoothly against the scuff marks on the carpet and his hand was on the doorknob by the time the second knock began. His other hand was ready for whatever was outside.

He pulled the door open several inches and snapped: "Who is it?"

Another bellhop stood outside, his hand still raised for knocking.

"Sir, excuse me," said an obsequious voice. "The porter Amos—may I speak to him?"

"By all means speak to him," snapped Nick, "but don't bother me about it. If you mean the fellow who brought my bag up, he left some time ago. Now if you don't mind..." He glanced down at his bare chest and tried to look as though he'd been disturbed in the middle of changing. The man's gaze travelled up the arm that loosely held the doorframe and stopped on the inside of Nick's right elbow. His eyes clung to the little blue axe-shaped tattoo that had been a part of Nick ever since he'd joined AXE years before.

"Is there something else?" Nick asked, impatient but polite.

"Oh! Are you sure he's gone, sir. He's needed for..."

"Of course I'm sure! Do you think I'm hiding him?"

The bellhop laughed ingratiatingly. "I'm sorry, sir; naturally not, sir." He peered into the room beyond Nick's outstretched arm before stepping back and bobbing his head. "Sorry to have bothered you, sir."

Nick closed the door and double-locked it quietly.

The phone rang. He scooped it up and barked into it irritably.

"I say, we're touchy today," a cheerful voice said into his ear. "What's new?"

"What could be new" he snapped back. "For God's sake. I just got here! What're you calling about?"

"About the meeting." The voice sounded hurt. "Is it on."

"Of course it's on. At headquarters, and don't be late. In fact, be there early if you can. I want to talk to you before the others get there. And for the luvva Pete, be on the ball with those minutes, will you?"

"Yes, *sir,*" the voice said crisply. "May I remind you that it's not necessary to pull rank with me, *sir.*" The caller rang off abruptly.

Nick replaced the receiver with a grin and moved to the windows to admire—and size up—the view.

His room was on the seventh floor. The morning traffic

roared busily beneath him. There were no projections anywhere on the smooth wall. The windows were far enough apart to make a visit from an adjoining room hazardous if not impossible. He latched them to be sure and closed the shutter-blinds.

His visitors awaited him on the bathroom floor.

The bellhop's body revealed one interesting item: a healthy bundle of Senegalese spending money. Nick counted it quickly and decided that it was worth a good three months of honest work or maybe a few minutes of something more spectacular—like knocking off a snoop.

The other man was different.

His upper body was scarred and pitted with tattoo marks similar to those on his face except that they were bigger and bulged outward in wormlike ridges. Some dirt or dye substance had been rubbed into the wounds while they were raw and had been sealed in, a score of years before, beneath the healing scars. A tribal custom, Nick knew. Performed by rite—but just exactly where? The marks were strange to him.

So was the dried root in the pouch that dangled from the cord around the man's neck. It was forked, like the mandrake root, and when he pressed it between his fingers it gave off a strange odour. But it was smaller than the typical mandrake and greyish-blue in colour. And the odour? Nick remembered: In the filthy room above the herbalist's shop—blood, alcohol, and . . . heroin. Heroin! That was it. But this, this was something very different. It was a pretty effective narcotic and a very powerful charm.

By the time the second knock sounded at the door Nick had washed and changed and was wishing that he'd had more than coffee on the plane. But this looked like another day in which he'd miss his breakfast.

He opened the door with his usual care after hearing the unusual rap that spelled out—though the caller didn't realize it—"Lizzie Borden took an axe . . ." and stared out at his visitor.

"Yes? What is it?" he snapped.

His new visitor darted a look down the passage and quickly lifted a corner of the handsome rubber mask he was wearing.

"It is I, Hakim the Hideous," he hissed. "With a new shipment of feelthy pictures."

Nick grinned and let him in.

"I have a grubby job for you," he said, and locked the door.

It took them only minutes to make their plans. Hakim would check into a nearby room and under cover of night would move the bodies into it and then check out. Ambassador Carter would stay at the Senegal as long as was convenient and then ostensibly fly back to Abimako.

Hakim studied the bodies. With his fleshlike mask pulled on top of his head, he looked more like a nightmare than ever.

"The root and the marks..." he murmured thoughtfully. "Together they are found in only one place—the hill country north of Abimako. We go there, perhaps?"

"Undoubtedly," said Nick. "When you've told me more about it. And when I'm finished in Dakar."

"And that will be when?" Hakim's good eye questioned him.

"When I've seen what's hopping at the Hop Club and what's so high about the 'high life' at the Kilimanjaro."

A HOP, A SKIP AND A SLUMP

Before Nick left he attached an extra lock to his bedroom door, one that AXE's specialists guaranteed to withstand everything short of a battering ram. He revealed its secret to Hakim who could then come and go as he wished and yet not leave the room and its grisly contents unguarded.

Ambassadors had to be very careful what they left lying around in their hotel rooms.

Hakim had certain arrangements to make and Nick went on his way without asking unnecessary questions. He couldn't help thinking, though, that the crosseyed Egyptian was singularly undismayed by the problems involved in the tactful disposal of corpses. In fact, the pleasure with which he approached his task was almost ghoulish.

"You can't do it alone," Nick had said. "Leave them until I get back from . . ."

"Never mind, never mind," Hakim interrupted. "You attend to your part of the job and I'll attend to mine. I can assure you that I shall handle it to your satisfaction. And to my own." And he had actually rubbed his hands together and cackled with villainous glee.

"Cornball," said Nick, and set to work effecting some striking changes in his own appearance.

Hakim had inspired him. When Nick left the Hotel Senegal, as unobtrusively as only he (and probably Hakim) knew how, he was already employing a shambling stride that looked slow and careless but covered the ground quickly. By the time he had gone two blocks he was sure that no one was following him or could possibly recognize him as the distinguished diplomat come to Dakar on grave, official business. He caught sight of himself in a shop window and almost gagged. Great! But let's not overdo it, Carter, or you'll be arrested on suspicion of something unspeakable.

He was nothing more sinister than a man with a pleasantly ugly face and a slight limp when he did the first part of his shopping and then checked into the Hotel Majestic under an indecipherable Polish name. He felt more comfortable the moment he had done it. This business of going around with his own name tied to his own face while he was engaged in a sticky job was something he hadn't cared for since his early days with the OSS. It was more a question of security than personal safety; the job couldn't help suffering when you were too easily recognized.

The rest of his shopping took him considerably more time and cost him more money, even though his purchases were very small. He hid them on himself, then bought a street map and made a tour of various sections of the city in case he found himself running up an unfamiliar alley pursued by cops or killers. In no time at all he had grounded himself at the wrong end of a *cul-de-sac*.

The Hop Club started hopping towards the end of the afternoon. Nick knew this because he had wandered past it and through the nearby streets during his tour, and read the sign that said: "OPEN 5 TIL????"

It was not much of a club as far as the entertainment was concerned. A scrawny piano player with huge, dilated eyes plinked away with a languid proficiency that might have sounded fine if the piano hadn't been dead and exhumed after a long interment. It also wasn't the kind of club with a uniformed doorman or a dues-paying membership—nearly all its clients seemed to be members of one desolate fraternity.

The Club served snack suppers and coffee, soft drinks and sandwiches, ice cream and alcohol. On the whole it was a pretty horrible—and very popular—place.

The piano moaned away while Nick stood just inside the doorway and looked around. His face was at its most repulsive and his skulking manner at its most obnoxious. Any right-thinking bouncer would have thrown him out at once. But the only guy who seemed to qualify as a bouncer eyed him without undue curiosity. There was neither major-domo nor hostess to show him to a table, and the male cashier made it clear that it wasn't his job to play escort to the suckers. The seedy waiters steadfastly ignored him.

Nick found a small table for himself, one near the door that gave him a fair view down the length of the room. It was a two-seater, pushed against the wall and far enough away from the nearest table to let a couple talk in peace if they wanted privacy.

But most of the couples weren't talking very much. Most of them weren't even couples. There were fewer women than men at the tables, and they were scarcely bargains at any price. Only one or two of them looked like anything other than leftovers. It was not so much their features that repelled as their thick, poorly applied make-up, and the tangled untidiness of their hair and clothes. At least half of the people wore dark glasses even in the poor light of the unclubby club. Not many of them seemed to be drinking very much. One man was singing and shouting to himself over a cup of coffee and several others seemed to be sipping the same stuff, only more quietly. Of course it was pretty early for the action to begin, but this lot didn't seem to be craving action. One group was talking and gesturing animatedly, but the others just sat around and twitched.

Christ Almighty, Nick thought, trying to grab a waiter. If Abe Jefferson had a place like this under his nose in Abimako he'd close it up in three seconds flat or else he'd have his own man sitting in on it. Which led to the thought that maybe the Dakar chief did, too.

The waiters continued to ignore him but somehow Nick began to feel noticed. Someone was definitely taking a good long look at him from the half-open service door in the back. He pulled a switch-knife out of his pocket and gave them something to look at. The blade clicked open so crisply that a man two tables over jumped and cringed away. Nick picked intently at his fingernails. It was not one of his favourite habits, but it gave him a chance to show off some minor hardware.

At last a reedy waiter in flowing off-white favoured him with a glance.

"Scotch," Nick snarled.

The waiter curled his lip. "Brandy and gin."

"Thanks for the suggestion, but I said Scotch."

"Only brandy and gin."

"All right, for Chrissake. Brandy and gin."

The waiter gave him the look that waiters specialize in and stalked off to the small bar opposite the piano. He came back with two shot glasses. One of brandy, one of gin.

"Shall I mix it?" he said insolently.

"I'll mix it," Nick growled. "And tell the manager I want to see him. Business."

The waiter raised one eyebrow. "I'll find out if it's convenient. What kind of business?"

Nick's eyes narrowed and his mouth became a thin, hard line.

"I'll tell him myself. Just get him." The malevolence in his face and the ice in his voice were not wasted. The man turned abruptly and walked to the door in the rear.

The gin was awful but the brandy was surprisingly smooth. Nick drank them both, swallowing the gin like medicine but lingering over the brandy. He pretended not to see the waiter stopping to exchange confidences with the bouncer, and looked pointedly at the radium dial of his watch. The bouncer—a bruiser in a bulging American suit—nodded and went in to deliver the message himself.

Nick was reaching into his pocket for the pack of Moroccan cigarettes he'd bought earlier in the day when the inner door opened wide and closed firmly. Nick concentrated on lighting up, forcing himself not to swing his head and stare and wondering how surprised it was politic for him to be.

The floor shook near him.

He let himself look up.

An immensity of female flesh wallowed to a stop beside his table. It was dressed in a vast and shapeless black thing that had to be a dress because it wasn't anything else, and it was one bulging roll of fat after another from the improbable ankles to the melon cheeks. Little piggy eyes peered at him from between the folds of face-fat, and huge earrings descended from the pendulous ear lobes. There were white, grandma ruffles at the sausage neck and lacy frills at the hem of the black sack. The incredibly dainty fingers of both chubby hands were dripping with rings. The small round mouth opened and a sound emerged from hiding.

"I am the manager," it mooed. "What is your business with me?"

Nick pushed back his chair but did not rise. He reached into an inner pocket and pulled out a card case.

"You're the manager? I didn't expect—uh—a woman. My card."

The moo turned into a bray of laughter. The great body shook and heaved like a mountain in an earthquake.

"That's not all you didn't expect, is it, meanface? What's this card?" She snatched at it with her bejewelled fingers and went on chuckling hugely. A scene from Coney Island flashed into Nick's mind, of the huge and madly laughing female who used to sit in her vast chair outside one of the amusement tunnels, rocking back and forth and exhorting customers to come in and thrill to the wild fun of the crazy mirrors and the rocketing cars and the things that popped up screaming from the cob-webby darkness. She had been carried off one day, still laughing, by the men in white coats and she had died in an insane asylum.

"A. Sigismondi!" she read out incredulously. "That's not your name, is it? It's not anybody's name!"

"Maybe it isn't," Nick admitted. "But I use it. Is there some place we can talk in private?"

"Novelties and Specialities," she read. "Casablanca."

"For God's sake," Nick murmured. "Not so loud. I didn't come here to talk to the whole damn room—just you."

Her small eyes stared into his face. "We'll talk here."

"I don't like it," Nick said flatly. "Maybe I better talk directly to the owner."

"You don't have to like it," she said, just as flatly. "And I *am* the owner. What are these specialities of yours? And why tell me about them?"

"I heard about your place in Casablanca," he said softly. "And my contacts tell me that you might be interested in what I have to offer. That is to say, they referred me to the Hop Club, but not to you by name. They are discreet. I hope that you are, too. Now perhaps you will let me talk to you without an audience."

She peered down at him, her eyes bright and penetrating.

"The Big One sent you?" she murmured.

He stared back at her, trying to look treacherous and reproving at the same time. "I know nothing of the Big One," he said, wishing that he did. "My business is my own. Except, of course, for my . . . associates in other countries."

"Ah, other countries." She flicked out a chair as though it had been made of matchsticks and scrunched down upon it. Her body and the chair groaned simultaneously. "You have samples of your novelties with you? They *must* be small enough to be hidden by my body!" She laughed hugely. "If we are going to talk, we must call each other something. I am Madame Sophia. Sophia, like Sophia Loren!" Her body rippled with enjoyment. "But how can I call you Sigismondi? It is impossible!"

"Call me anything you like," he said shortly. "Let's not waste each other's time. First give my card back, if you please, and then make no move until I have shown you what I have. If you are not interested, say so, and I will leave. But I warn you, Madame Sophia, when I go I do not intend to be interferred with by your hired hands." His expression was concentrated menace.

She pierced him with her bright, tiny eyes and pushed the card to him across the table. One sleeve slid inches up her fat arm and he saw the pinpricks. At least she wouldn't holler for the cops. "You are hard," she whinnied approvingly. "I like a ruthless man. These others are—pah!" Disdain shivered through her body. "You have strength. Show me what else you have." Her tone and her glance were so suggestive that she seemed to be talking of things other than the samples in his pocket.

He hid his feeling of revulsion and looked away from her at the two new customers coming in. They belonged in dark, dockside alleys, or at some Mau Mau campfire, mouthing horrible oaths and thrusting their clawed hands into living human entrails; or they belonged to the Hop Club and whatever organization collected degenerate beings and turned them into murderers.

Nick watched them find a table in the rear before pulling the first of the packets out of his pocket. At the same time he noticed several other men leaving their tables and shambling through the door beyond the skinny piano player.

He hunched his shoulders and leaned down over the table, shielding the packet from all eyes but her's. His hand bared it but did not let go. It was transparent plastic, filled with a white powder more sought after and carrying a higher price tag than gold dust, even though it had been cut and sliced and powdered by one soulless thief after another. She would never know this until she tried it—and he hadn't brought it here for anyone to use.

"I have more of that," he murmured. "Much more. Bigger packets, many of them, worth millions if I could reach the American market. But this is more convenient for me—especially if I can unload in quantity. Understand, I do not have to. I know of other markets. And I will go to them if you are not interested."

"Let me open it," she breathed.

"Here?" Nick hissed. "You must be mad. You must have an office or back room we can use."

Madame Sophia looked from him to the packet.

"Perhaps we can," she cooed. "Perhaps. You had something else to show me?"

He slid the packet away from her grasping fingers and reached inside his packet for the second of the two most vital items he had managed to secure during the day.

It was tube-shaped more or less, and smaller than his hand, so that concealing it on its trip across the table-top was easy. He opened his hand in front of her and her huge breasts drooped down to meet it.

He heard a tiny gasp coming from the elephantine frame.

"Where did you get this?" Her fat but dainty fingers pinched at the root and squeezed obscenely.

Nick shrugged. "What difference does it make, if you have a use for it?"

Her tiny mouth pursed. "There is not much use for only one."

Nick clicked his tongue impatiently. "One! I told you these are samples. I have unlimited supplies."

"That is most unlikely," Madame Sophia said sceptically. "I know the source of these things, and I know that they grow only under very rare conditions. Your supplies cannot possibly be unlimited. You are lying."

Nick filled his voice with impatience and contempt.

"You know the source! When it has only been discovered by *my people* within the last few weeks? Pah! I suppose you are referring to that dried-up vegetable patch in—what's the place's name—that place in the Nyanga hills."

"Duolo," she said thoughtfully. "So. Dried-up vegetable patch. Hmm. Yes, I think we can come to terms. We will go to my rooms in the back." She heaved and grunted her way up from the chair. Nick put the samples into his inside pockets and significantly patted a hidden holster. "No tricks, now," he warned. "I don't give up anything for nothing."

"Why should you?" she mooed understandingly. "Come."

It seemed to him that there was no sound in the room but the tinny tinkle of the piano and the creaking of the floor beneath her feet. And it felt as though every eye in the room was boring into him.

Madame Sophia made a reassuring gesture to the brawny bouncer and waddled majestically through the inner door with Nick trailing in her wake. She led the way down a narrow passage barely large enough to let her through, grazing past several closed doors and one slightly open one. Nick paused behind her to light up one of his Casablanca cigarettes and dart a swift look in through the crack. What he saw and heard in that brief flash of time was worth his entire trip.

A bland-faced young man in a bright American shirt was talking into a radio transmitter. His face was the typical yellow-beige of China, and his voice was pure Chinese American. It was saying: "... success is ours if the president dies. Our cause goes well ..."

Nick caught up silently with Madame Sophia and followed her into a room at the end of the passage.

She closed the door behind them.

"My office," she said.

It was some office. It was furnished with an immense desk, immense chairs, and an immense bed.

"Sit, and let us talk."

Nick chose a straight-backed chair and sat down. For some reason his cigarette tasted foul and there was an unaccountable queasiness at the pit of his stomach. He looked around for an ashtray and stubbed out the cigarette.

"I want it understood," he said, "that I'm in this business *because* it's business, and that's all. I can supply as much as you need whenever you need it. There is of course a delivery charge that's added to the sale price." Nausea almost overwhelmed him and dizziness flooded his head.

"Ah, delivery charge," murmured Madame fatly. "But you look a little pale. A drink, perhaps?"

A drink! Sweet Jesus, that was it! Never take a chance on a stranger in a place like this—never. A mickey, a quick frisk, then either truce or death.

"No thanks," he said. "That gin was poison. You're right, I don't feel good. Think I'll get some fresh air." He staggered to his feet.

Madame Sophia laid her fat little right hand on his arm and squeezed. "Why don't you just lie down until you feel better? Sleep a little. Rest." She tugged at him suggestively, manoeuvring him towards the bed. The old elephant had muscle hidden beneath that fat, he thought dazedly. Got to get out of here. Got to get out of here. They'll see through disguise. Find weapons Wilhelmina Hugo Pierre see AXE tattoo take heroin and dump me.

He took a deep breath and shook her hand off.

"No," he snarled. "You think I'm crazy. You'll be sorry for this filthy trick."

"Why, sweetie," she cooed. "I don't know what you mean by trick. Come, now, lie down on the bed." Her strength seemed to be growing while his faded. It was hopeless; he had to go before he blanked out altogether.

He sank one fist into her great belly. She gave a belching gasp and clutched herself without falling. Christ! She was whale blubber and rhino hide and giant sandbag all rolled into one. One fat hand reached for an alarm button near the desk and the other scrabbled at his throat. The O-shaped mouth and pouter-pigeon chest were gathering for a scream. Nick drew back his failing right arm and slammed the hard side of his hand against that ugly mouth and up at the button nose. This time Madame grunted and staggered back, blood spurting from her nose. It seemed an eternity before she dropped, but drop she did. Nick planted one more vengeful blow in the vast abdomen and stumbled to the "office" door.

How the hell get out of this place before he dropped in his tracks... His head was swinging like a yo-yo and his legs were turning to spaghetti.

Wilhelmina came out of her holster as Nick swung open the door and shuffled into the passage. She was noisy, but she was his best bet under these conditions. Wilhelmina was a 9mm stripped-down Luger who had done time in the SS Barracks at Munich before Nick had killed her owner and adopted her. She had become his most trustworthy troubleshooter.

A wave of sickness came over him, and he moaned. The door to the radio room swung open and the operator stepped out and stared at him. So soon! Nick moaned to himself. One shot here and the whole house is down upon me and I don't even know how to get out of here.

He leapt at the blurred colours of the plaid shirt and drew back Wilhelmina with all his strength. Wilhelmina struck quietly but with a force as deadly as her bullets, dealing the blow to the throat that crushes the windpipe, and delivering it with lethal power and precision.

The fellow in the plaid shirt managed one awful noise and dropped. Suddenly all the doors down the passage flew open and it seemed that the floor swayed and the whole length of the narrow hallway was a gauntlet filled with scarecrow creatures with goggling eyes and clutching, clawing hands.

SOMETHING OLD, SOME NEW

WILHELMINA wavered in his faltering grasp. The impossibly big eyes of the human scarecrows swam before Nick's face.

He gritted his teeth and swore bitterly to himself. Goddamn you Carter pull yourself together and get out get out get out! A hand plucked at his sleeve. He pulled his arm away angrily as if he'd been jostled by a beggar in a crowd, and the feebleness of his own gesture alarmed him so much that a little shiver of awareness ran through him and his eyes pulled briefly into focus. Nick tightened his grip on Wilhelmina and willed his feet to walk in a straight, agonized line down the narrow passage. As he walked he whispered, like a man in his own dream or someone else's nightmare.

"One move out of any one of you," he crooned maliciously, only dimly conscious of what he was saying, "and I shoot. One sound, one tiny move, one step in any direction..." Wilhelmina's one black eye scanned the hallway, probing back and forth, back and forth. "...and you die. Anybody want to die?" He reeled forward and the gaunt figures drew away from him without moving their feet, without moving their hands, just swaying back and watching him with their sick, frightened eyes. "Because whoever gets in my way is going to die." One foot, other foot, one foot, other foot, choke down the sickness and keep it in your stomach, half-close the eyes and keep them in your head, blink away the blackness, pinch your brain to stay awake... The passage forked. One fork led back to the café. The other probably led to the rear and a door to the street. But maybe not.

"You. You." Wilhelmina jabbed at a tattered sleeve. "Which way outa here? Show me. Lead the way."

A frightened junkie tried to backtrack into his cubicle. Nick snarled and prodded him with the Luger. "Come on! Show me! And not the front. The back." The man shook convulsively, but managed a shambling turn towards the left and into another short passage with a door at the end of it. Nick plodded after him, fighting to keep his mind alert amidst the red haze that swirled around it.

"Open that door. Tell me if there's anyone outside. Don't lie—I'll blow your head off."

Trembling fingers fumbled at the knob. The door swung open. Nick's unwilling escort shot him one burning look of hatred and stepped outside.

"No one," he reported. "People end of block, not here."

Nick loomed up behind him and pressed Wilhelmina into the gaunt back. He stared dazedly out into the street. Seemed clear, so far as he could see through the thick, painful mist that was almost drowning him. A door opened some feet or yards behind him and through the roaring in his ears he heard a strangled shout or perhaps it was nothing but a sharp intake of breath. He pushed past the fellow in the doorway with such surprising force that the man stumbled and fell with a sharp, sibilant curse. Nick sucked in the late afternoon air and willed his feet into a run. They were lead, and he was living death, and his senses screamed at him to give up the unequal battle and let the red darkness swallow him. But the one glowing spark that was his sixth sense told him that he must run and dodge and run again, because danger ran behind him and he could not let himself go down or else . . . or else . . . or else what? He felt dimly that the end of the world would come if he gave in, and it would be all his fault. A gust of wind slapped lightly at his face, lending him fleeting strength. His dulled hearing caught the sound of footsteps much too near him and he darted a glance over his shoulder. The footsteps slowed and Nick's half-focused eyes saw the man with the green face and the froggy lids raise an arm, thrust it down between its own shoulder blades and come up with something long that glinted ominously.

Instinct welled up from some hidden depth and made Nick fire even as he twisted his unwilling body to one side. A long, wicked knife sang past him to clatter uselessly to the sidewalk; the man called Laszlo yelped and clutched his shattered shoulder. Nick fired again and saw Green Face throw himself down into the street and scrabble crabwise into an open doorway. My God! Was that doorway still so close? Nick forced himself upright and stumbled into a run, pumping one more useless shot over his shoulder.

It seemed to him that there was a thundering of feet from somewhere behind him, somewhere behind Laszlo, somewhere in that crazy house with all the doors and cubicles. He made his tired mind pump sparks of energy into his heavy body, and he ran.

His mental map shimmered, blurred out, re-formed into the small blocks, side streets, broad avenues and twisting alleys that he'd scouted so painstakingly hours or weeks or years before. He ran like one possessed forgetting that the clever fugitive won't run but blend into his surroundings, remembering only that he must follow his planned route of escape. His heart was pounding harder than his footsteps, and his stumbling feet were enemies of speed and caution. At last he found the archway and the unpaved lane he sought. A tall man in a flowing blue robe stared at him as he entered, but made no move to stop him.

Nick staggered through the lane and came out into narrow back street lined with shacks that were little more than straw-hut dwellings. He crossed it in a loping run that seemed to him no more than a crawl, and when he reached the other side he tripped on the low walk and fell.

Peace. Rest. It was wonderful. He lay face down and felt his mind drifting, drifting...No! Get up and go! Get up, you goddamn legs move! Open, bastard eyes, and stay open! He drew a deep, painful breath, then another and another, calling on his last resource of Yoga-trained strength and will to pull himself off the littered sidewalk and back on to his feet.

His leaden legs ran painfully for one more block and took him to a wider street that led into a noisy, pungent market place busy with the evening trade. Nick slowed to a walk and lumbered into the crowd like a man wallowing through muddy water. He threaded his uncertain way through groups of veiled Tuaregs and tanned, proud featured Moors, past the flower stalls and the displays of exquisite silverware and bizarre amulets, away from whatever hunted for him in the narrow back streets. Stopping at a stall that steamed with hot foods and hotter liquids, he bought a mug of sweet, strong coffee and made himself look back for pursuers. If they were still after him, he could no longer see them. The coffee scalded a path down his throat and into his stomach. He drank as much as he could bear of the hot, sweet stuff and then moved on. Across the square and down the block. Across the street and down another. He saw a battered taxi bustling by and longed to hail it. But it passed him by before he managed to raise an arm to flag it. The red haze settled back into his head and pressed down on his shoulders. Walk! he told himself fiercely. Walk damn you, and keep on walking.

At last the heavy legs that seemed to belong to some recalcitrant robot took him to broad streets lined with shining pink and blue houses; past the houses and their flowered balconies to the wide business streets; past the statues in a city square; past the small Parisian stores and into a street that gave him a message of comfort and familiarity.

It was impossible to manage the last few steps between the corner and the welcome, open doors of the Majestic. A man could only do so much, and then his poisoned body had to rest or drop...

A shout sounded behind him. It was like the gust of

wind that had helped to galvanize him once before. Then huge Senegalese soldiers strode down the sidewalk ahead; he summoned enough strength to dart in front of them, forcing himself to maintain a steady stride so that they remained behind him as a human shield until he reached the hotel doors.

A newspaper was the last thing in the world that he wanted at the moment but he forced himself to stop at the lobby news-stand while he waited to see if anyone came after him. Three lady tourists and a naval officer wandered in. He went upstairs without asking for his key and let himself in with his own door opener. The bed was soft . . . comfortable . . . treacherously inviting . . . Nick turned down the invitation and called Room Service He paced the floor until the coffee came. Then he double-locked the door and drank and probed his throat with a shaking finger and drank some more and retched. He walked and drank and walked and probed and poured his insides out into the bathroom until a more natural tiredness overtook him. And then, at last he let himself sit down and rest.

Special Ambassador Nicholas Carter stepped briskly into the Hotel Senegal shortly after the late sunset and the sudden onslaught of dark night, making no attempt to hide or disguise his arrival but not precisely flaunting himself for the benefit of bomb throwers or other possible assassins. He walked across the lobby with the crowd and he waited until his elevator was almost full before he entered it. A laughing young couple got out with him and stopped three doors before his own, partially blocking the view of the watcher at the opposite end of the hallway but giving Nick a chance to see himself being watched.

He rapped the "Lizzie Borden" signal on his door before releasing the two locks—the standard fixture, and his own—and entering, his mind on Hakim and various other people and his hand on Wilhelmina.

Hakim tossed aside his newspaper as Nick entered.

"Ah! The wanderer returns, looking a trifle pale. May I recommend to you a medicinal portion of your very excellent Scotch?"

Nick noticed the glass on the table beside his crosseyed colleague and he saw that Hakim had been concealing a formidable snub-nosed weapon behind his newspaper. He reset the door locks and nodded enthusiastically.

"You can. You can even pour it. Is the man down the hallway something to do with you, or does he come with the hotel?"

Hakim looked up from pouring and glanced at Nick sharply with his one good eye. "So he's still there, is he? No, he is not mine."

"But he's seen you coming and going, huh? Thanks." Nick swallowed gratefully and lowered himself into an easy chair. "And he knows you have access to the room even when I'm not here?"

"I'm not sure he does." Hakim flung himself comfortably into his chair. "I made great play of knocking and being let in by you, and I think I had him fooled until you came back. He must be feeling quite confused by now."

Nick grinned. "Maybe we ought to give him even more to think about by luring him in here and inviting him to talk. But I doubt if he's got much to offer."

Hakim made a face and nodded. "It would be an entertainment, certainly, but he has the look of a rather stupid underling and he may as well stay out there as be replaced by a tougher customer. Perhaps it is best for me to handle him tonight with our other departing friends." He jerked his evil head in the direction of the closed bathroom. "Unless you think he will make difficulties for you when you leave here again?"

"I'll manage. Now what about your arrangements for the evening? All set?"

The incredibly ugly face contrived a look even more appalling than usual. "Ah, yesss!" the cockeyed one hissed with hideous glee. "The bodies move tonight!"

Nick raised his eyebrows questioningly. "Of their own volition, no doubt? May I ask . . .?"

"No, friend, you may not. Evil genius must have its secrets. By the way, I have good news. The grapevine tells me that President Makombe has passed the crisis and shows every sign of making a good recovery."

"Thank God for that," Nick said sincerely. "That means we have some hope of cleaning up this mess. But what's your contact with the grapevine? I thought you weren't known in these parts?"

Hakim closed his good eye in a mysterious wink and let the other stare up at the ceiling. "I have my methods. Now perhaps instead of asking me all these awkward questions you will tell me how you spent your day and why you look so pale and interesting."

Nick told him, in brief but vivid detail. Hakim listened with growing interest and made little sucking sounds of appreciation.

"Allah and all his little ones be praised!" he said admiringly. "You must have a head that would bend bullets. But what a pity that we could not call on Honest Abe to raid that stinkhole and flush out all the rats."

"Yeah, well, the only one who got flushed out was me," Nick said sourly. Then he smiled reflectively. "I did make one anonymous phone call on my way here—to the local cops. Actually it wasn't quite anonymous. I mooed at them hysterically and told them that my name was Madame Sophia and that there'd been a murder at my innocent establishment, the Hop Club. Would they hurry, please, because the murderer was still about and had even attempted an assault on *me*, Sophia. Then I screamed and hung up rapidly." Hakim's face split into its incongruously attractive grin. "I don't know what good it'll do." Nick concluded, "but at least it should harass them. And a little harassment can sometimes be a very handy thing."

"I must say you're a most unusual Ambassador." Hakim's tone conveyed both compliment and query. "Is this the way you always conduct your delicate negotiations?"

"We diplomats must be adaptable," Nick said. "And you're not my idea of a typical professor. Let's have another drink."

They drank to the health of President Julian Makombe, and Nick changed into his evening clothes. He made a small adjustment on his cane, told Hakim to enjoy his evening's entertainment, and very quietly let himself out into the hallway.

The watcher was no longer at his post.

Nick frowned to himself. It suited him not to have to deal with the man but—where had he gone, and why? Nick's silent progress down the hall was even more circumspect than usual. But he was still alone when the elevator came, and just as much alone when he stepped into the car.

Except of course, for the elevator operator.

The doors closed silently behind him and he turned to face the front.

The operator took the car down less than one floor and pressed the stop button. The car shivered to a halt.

"Trouble?" Nick said mildly. But his every sense was tingling and alert.

"Much trouble," agreed the operator. Something metallic appeared in his hand and he turned to Nick. "The trouble is you die." The gun in his hand was equipped with the usual semi-silent silencer.

"I *what?* Are you mad?" Nick raised his cane as if involuntarily.

"You die," the man repeated implacably. "Striking me will not help you." He raised the gun.

"But *why?*" said Nick, and fired first. The metal sliver of death flew into the man's bare throat with the velocity of a bullet. The gun hand jerked upward as Nick leapt aside, and the strangled cry almost drowned out the popping sound of the wild bullet as it left the gun. The shot slammed high into the wall of the wood-panelled cage. And something went "ting! ting!" The elevator operator's knees buckled. He tore frantically at his throat, and dropped heavily. Only meticulous inspection would show how the man had died.

"Ting!"

Nick thought rapidly. He thrust the gun into his pocket and glanced at the numbered lights. Floors eleven, seven, five . . . ting! . . . and eight were calling. He stepped over the body and applied himself to the elevator switches.

The car started with a petulant grunt. Nick took it down to the third floor and prayed.

He stepped out into the carpeted hallway of the third

floor and breathed a sigh of relief. A waiter was intent on manoeuvring a service cart from a room several doors down, and apart from him nothing stirred in the hall. Nick kept his face turned away from the waiter and made for the stairway with casual haste. Then he took the remaining flights downstairs at a gallop.

The lobby stirred with nothing more than its usual activity.

Nick strolled through it and out into the night. A line of taxicabs was waiting at the curb.

He decided to walk. Fortunately, the Kilimanjaro was within easy strolling distance. For this he was grateful—he was in no mood for either unknown taxi drivers or marathon walks. And if Rufus Makombe's recommended place of entertainment was anything like his recommended hotel, Nick would be needing all the energy and wits he had.

It was a place with an unobtrusive exterior and simple furnishings. But it was big and airy, its customers were many cuts above the habitués of the Hop Club, and it throbbed with life.

Nick ordered wine and a selection of the "sample regional specialties" suggested by President Makombe's younger brother. The service was swift and cheerful, and both food and wine were excellent. A group of singers, accompanied by a fantastically versatile drum, was singing with youthful vitality laced with talent and the fresh sophistication of a new, exuberant world. The audience—black, white, cream-beige and darkly tanned, dressed to the nines or in the simplest of street clothes—tapped feet and clapped hands with a spontaneity that made Nick feel, for moments, as carefree as they were. It was an effort for Nick to remember that he had a job to do, although how the job could possibly tie in with this joyful place and crowd was still a mystery to him. But no doubt the mystery would clear if he stayed with it long enough.

The performers bowed and went their way to the sound of thunderous applause. Nick sipped his wine and waited.

All the lights went out. All the laughing stopped.

An invisible drum began to beat a slow insistent rhythm. It was quiet at first, as if coming from the distant hills, and then it grew nearer while its beat built into a pattern of urgency.

A low voice throbbed into being, met the drumbeat, murmured rings around it and soared high into the air as if there were no ceiling but only open sky above. It hung there for a long moment, sweet and clear as a wild bird's song, and then it fell gently in a series of low sighs like a river flowing downstream over small, smooth stones.

It seemed to Nick that a sigh shivered through the darkened room. It blew through him like a breeze in a forest of young trees, and he felt his blood run hot and cold. A dim light, at first no more than the glow of a torchlight in a mist, softened the darkness in the centre of the room. It grew gradually as the voice soared and sang in words that were strange but in sounds that told of remembered sorrows and dark valleys, of jungle creatures and cool lakes and sunlit mountain tops and new loves and primitive passions. As the torchlight grew into full light it showed a woman with her arms outstretched, a tall woman with a crown of night-black hair and a face that men would dream of till they died, a full-bodied, full-blooded woman, whose exquisite form swayed and trembled with the passion of her song. She shimmered and burned so brightly with the light of her own sensual beauty that she put the artificial light to shame.

The houselights lowered to a candle glow. The song faded down to join the drum and stayed with it. A whisper of male voices rose from somewhere in the darkness. The whisper grew into a word breathed by a chorus, and the one word was her name. "Mirella . . . Mirella . . . Mirella . . ." The chorus faded like a breath of wind. The drumbeat quickened.

Mirella danced. Her own voice and the single drum were her accompaniment; the dance began with a slow quivering of muscles and built into an ecstasy. And while she danced she was the centre of the earth and all eyes in the room caressed her. Her own eyes sought nothing; they had already found it. Her eyes, her movements and her pulsating voice were concentrating on one being.

She was looking only at Nick.

He was mesmerized by her.

There was a magnetism about her that was almost supernatural. But there was nothing supernatural about her perfectly formed limbs or the way they moved. It was not a dance so much as a suggestion, and not a song so much as an intimate invitation. Intimate, subtle, unmistakable and irresistible.

Nick felt her spell bewitching him and found himself incapable of fighting it off, of even wanting to fight. His will melted as he gazed at her, absorbing her compelling beauty with all his senses. Her luminous, hypnotic eyes, all the more dazzling for the kohl-touched lids, caught his and wrapped them up.

The drumbeat and her palpitating movements changed again. This time she spoke in a lovely liquid accent he found hard to place, though the burnished copper of her skin suggested both North Africa and the Middle East. She would sing, she said, of warriors and a lion hunt, of how they tracked and ran and speared and fought until at last they returned in triumph to their homes, panting from their labours.

At first her lithe movements and the low throbbing of her voice suggested stealth and caution. Gradually they built into the intensity of the hunt and then the kill, and her voice soared to incredible heights before ending with a shuddering sigh. Her feet stamped lightly in a sort of triumph and her hips twitched rhythmically while her breath gasped out its message of exhaustion. Nick had seen young warriors at the end of hunting and he knew her artistry was incredible; and yet to him the movements were not only suggestive of the climax of a hunt but also of a climax far more sensual and ecstatic. At last she closed her eyes and let her arms and head fall back as if into a sleep, and a contented smile played about her lips. Then she was no longer warrior but a woman dreaming of her lover. Her arms rose languidly and began to caress her own body. A veil floated lightly to the floor.

Nick was conscious for the first time of what she was

wearing, and even then he could not have described it. It was something shimmering and yet diaphanous when she raised her arms against the lights. It was full, yet moulded to her body; and instead of being the single flowing garment he at first thought it was, it was a multiplicity of separate folds and veils. One by one they floated free, and the lovely body swayed and gyrated. A little pulse hammered in Nick's temple. The woman was incredible; voluptuous without vulgarity, giving of her beauty without shame but not shamelessly; impersonal, almost mysterious, yet warm and infinitely desirable. Somehow all the Yoga training in the world failed Nick at this moment. Breath control be damned! he thought, and felt himself come close to panting.

She looked at him again through long, thick lashes, and he thought he saw a smile that was meant for him alone. Perhaps they all thought that. But he also felt a sense of his own destiny, and knew that she was part of it.

The longest veil wafted to the floor. The drumbeat quickened and the long, lovely hips quickened with it. Another and another twitch of filmy cloth and gracefully spasmodic movement...and she was almost naked in all her female glory. The houselights died silently and the one big beam began to dim. She stretched out her arms imploringly in a gesture that could have meant she'd had enough, or wanted much, much more. Then she tore the last strips off her body almost savagely. An animal grunt swept through the house. For a fractional beat of time she stood there with her magnificent body completely bared and almost still but for a tiny muscular quivering that was far more provocative than the most blatant of sexual gestures; and then the light went out.

Nick felt the breath go out of him like air out of a balloon and he knew from the gusty sounds around him that every red-blooded male in the place was having the same reaction. He felt oddly jealous.

A saxophone crooned into the darkness and the lights came on one by one. Mirella and all her veils had gone. A thumping, clapping, cheering audience demanded her return, but Mirella, said the giant Senegalese emcee, did no encores. One act like hers was all any man deserved, he said, and rolled his eyes. The males in the audience cheered.

The small band was good and a little dark-skinned crooner sang the latest hits from Ghana, the lyrics of which were apparently packed with sly meaning and good humour. Gradually, Mirella's exotic aura faded and a hundred male dreams melted in the air. Feet tapped, hands clapped, full glasses clinked.

Nick felt deflated. The Ghanaian songs were fun, but they had nothing on Mirella. Her spell still lingered over him. It was a long time since he had felt so completely captivated by any woman, so painfully drawn to such overwhelming beauty and desirability. He wondered how he could manage to meet her—send his diplomatic compliments perhaps, and would she join him in a drink? But why had she looked at him like that? If in fact she had. He thought it over. Yes, she *had* been looking at him. Maybe a message via a waiter would do the trick...

But the message came to him.

"Mr. Ambassador Carter, sir?"

Nick raised his eyebrows and nodded at the waiter before him.

"Miss Mirella sends her greetings, sir, and requests your kind presence in her dressing room. She would come out herself, but she prefers not to be stared at by all the people, if you don't mind, sir."

"Delighted," said Nick. "That's very kind of her. You'll show me . . . ?" He reached for his cane and rose.

"This way, sir."

Nick followed the man across the room and through a swinging double door to the backstage area. It was clean and cheerful and brightly lit, and he had none of the sense of foreboding that so often came when he stepped through strange doorways into back passages.

"Here, sir." The waiter stopped and tapped at a starred door.

"Come in."

Nick entered. The waiter closed the door quietly behind him and padded away.

Mirella rose from a soft settee against the wall and stretched out an arm in graceful greeting.

"Mr. Carter? I am very honoured."

Nick held her hand briefly but with warmth. "The honour is mine—and all the luck. To what do I owe it? And what do I call you?"

She smiled, and a chorus of slightly fallen angels sang. Her beauty was even more striking from so near at hand, but she was no wide-eyed innocent working her way through nursing school, nor was she the usual hardbitten bitch of the nightclub circuit. Everything was her own, from the lovely, knowing eyes to the slightly crooked teeth, from the smooth copper skin to the firm but supple flesh, and everything about her was breathtaking beauty that knew its way around but still thought the world a fine and lovely place. A place more for wild creatures than for human beings, perhaps, but still a place for joyous living and ecstatic loving.

"You call me Mirella. Please sit down." She gestured at the settee. "Perhaps you would like a drink more satisfying than our light wine?" A small cabinet came open at her touch. Nick noticed ice cubes and glasses waiting. "I almost live here, so I like to have refreshments for my friends. Cognac? Scotch? Irish whiskey? I even have some bourbon." She smiled again. Nick liked the slightly crooked teeth and the warmth that lit her eyes.

"Scotch. please," he said. "Save the bourbon and surprise some other guest."

"There'll be no other guests tonight," she answered. "And I haven't answered your first question." She paused for a moment while she poured two sturdy shots into the glasses and added just a touch of soda. "I asked you here for two reasons. One, because Rufus asked me to look out for a tall, distinguished-looking American with a cane who was doing all he could to find out what's troubling Nyanga; and two, I saw you watching me. You weren't—what is the word? yes—drooling, so I liked you. I do not often like the audience, even though the management is very strict about the clientele." She handed him a glass and sat down on the settee beside him. "To your success and health, Ambassador Carter."

She raised her glass and looked deep into his eyes. His

heart skipped one tiny beat and settled down to something close to normal.

"To yours," he said warmly. They drank.

Mirella . . . Mirella . . . Mirella . . . Was that what they called the wind? No, not quite. But they should have. She was a sultry summer breeze, a breath of spring—no, she wasn't. She was a siren on a rock, filling his ears with the music of her voice and turning his knees to jelly, a lovely Lorelei who was all woman from her dark hair to her toes.

They talked for a while, and then they stopped. He found himself staring at her face as if it were the one face in the world he'd ever wanted to be gazing at, and she looked back at him with something in her eyes that matched the pleasant tension of his body.

When they had stared for moments she lowered her eyes and turned her head away. Nick put his glass down and rose instantly.

"Don't let me outstay my welcome," he said longingly. "I'm sure you want to rest. I'll be on my way."

"Oh, no!" She got up and lightly touched his arm. "Don't go. I was wondering—you see, my day starts late, so for me it is still early. There are friends I must see tonight, friends of the Makombes, and I thought perhaps you . . . might care to come with me." Her dazzlingly lovely face looked into his, and there was something pleading in it. Nothing desperate, nothing of fear; something pleasantly urgent that struck a harmonious chord with what he felt himself.

"I'd love to," he murmured happily. The back of his mind said "I wonder where the body will be buried?" and all the rest of him shivered pleasurably and said "Oh my God, what a woman, what a woman!"

He helped her into her coat. It slid on smoothly over the gauzy gown that was so much like the one she'd stripped off in filmy pieces on to the floor.

"Thank you," she said. "Do you mind if we stop off at my place for a moment? They're the sort of people who sit outdoors at night and listen to the crickets; I'd like to change into something a little warmer. It won't take long —my apartment's on the way."

"Whatever you say. But I'm afraid I don't have a car."

"Mine's outside. Perhaps you'll drive." She flashed the wonderful smile at him again and took his arm. The warmth of even that small touch spread through him like a brush fire. He longed to kiss her. But even for Carter it was a couple of minutes too soon.

Singing from the big room followed them to the street, and that was all that did. Nick slid behind the wheel of the expensive year-old car and drove according to her murmured but concise directions. The uniformed gateman at her garden-apartment house greeted them with a smile and guaranteed to take care of the car until their return.

Mirella's apartment was Cairo modern, plus piles of soft, skin rugs and huge, deep cushions that served as chairs. She latched the door behind them and Nick parked his cane to help her off with her wrap.

"Where shall I put it?"

"Just toss it on the chair—I'll be needing it again in a few minutes."

He laid it down gently and turned into the richness of her living room. Mirella touched a switch and the dim light brightened almost imperceptibly. Muted colours came to life.

"It's lovely," he said, and meant it.

"Thank you. Drinks and ice are in here..." She brushed against him very lightly as she reached for the cabinet and opened it. Sensation shivered through his veins. She touched another switch and low, blue music filled the room almost instantly, making him tingle suddenly with its tantalizing magic. At least, something was making him tingle. Perhaps it was the way she moved. Or perhaps it was the way her breasts thrust against the filmy fabric that covered them without concealing their temptations. She turned towards him and he knew that, though the music added spice, it was she who was enchanting and she who made his senses whirl, she who had the exciting beauty of a youthful, uncalculating Cleopatra.

"But you're even lovelier," he said softly, and thought his voice sounded slightly choked. "And you must hear that so often that it bores you."

"No." Her luminous eyes traced a gentle pattern over his face. "It is not something I hear often. I only see the staring, and then I run. I run into a crowd of friends, and meet only *their* friends, who try not to stare but talk instead about the weather, and *then* it is that I am bored." The slight smile on her delectable lips was yet another temptation.

Nick lowered his eyes. "I'll do my very best to stare no more, and I can say with absolute honesty that I have no desire to talk about the weather. I *do* want to say that you are the most beautiful and bewitching woman I have ever seen. And the funny thing is, you're human. And I happen to be crazy about slightly crooked teeth. Now if you don't go and change I'll start gaping at you again and you'll throw me out."

She laughed, a low and happy sound. Her hand reached over and touched him under the chin, gently raising his head so that his eyes, inevitably, looked right down into hers, and his chin was resting on the soft velvet of her fingers.

"I wouldn't think of throwing you out. You look at me in a different way, as though you also see my face. And I like it. I like it. I love to be told that I am beautiful. *And* human!" Her hand released his chin and dropped to his shoulder. "I think that you are beautiful, too. Is that a funny thing to say to a man? Your face is strong and your eyes . . . they have depth. Cruelty and laughter and determination, that is what I see in them."

"It's admiration that you're seeing now," said Nick. "Perhaps you'd better not come any closer. Admiration has a way of turning into lust."

"So it has," she murmured. "Yes, perhaps you're right. I must go and change at once." But the move she made was still towards him, and then her other arm was resting on his shoulder. "And there is such strength about your mouth," she whispered, almost inaudibly. "I wonder if that can be cruel, too." Tall though she was for a woman, she had to raise herself on her toes to do what she wanted. Her lips brushed his and lingered lightly. Then the tip of her tongue ran lightly over his lips. Her eyes were half-closed as she said, "Not cruel at all. Too firm, perhaps. Unyielding. But flesh, not stone. Is it ever any softer?"

This time his lips found hers and his arms encircled her. His kiss was light at first, a soft caress and gentle savouring, but when he felt her mouth open under his and her tongue probe his tongue, he allowed himself to yield to his own need. His kiss became passionate and searching, and his mouth fused with hers. Yet he could not get enough, nor could she, and as they held the long, molten kiss their bodies moved closer until they clung as close together as two clothed bodies can.

She bent the spell at last, but did not break it, by turning away her head and sighing deeply. Nick fingered the loose knot of her rich dark hair.

"You shouldn't have let me do that," he breathed. "You've made me want too much. I want to kiss you all over... I want to take the clothes off you myself..."

Mirella raised her lovely head. "I want it, too," she whispered. "Kiss me again, and take them off."

His kiss was less lingering and more urgent than before. Then he slid the gossamer gown down past her shoulders and caught his breath again at the marvellous beauty of her.

"Please, you too," she said softly. "Undress with me—let me help you." Her graceful fingers plucked gently at his jacket and took it from him. The luminous eyes narrowed slightly when she saw Wilhelmina resting at the waistband of Nick's trousers. "You carry a gun?"

"Standard procedure," Nick said lightly. "In case of enemy action. I'm not always in the company of friends." He expertly removed one of her filmy undergarments.

"You are safe with me," she said quietly, and he believed her.

Strange, how wonderful the simple act of undressing could be, when Man undressed Woman and Woman undressed Man.

They did it gently, courteously, exploringly, until they stood before each other like Adam and Eve before the fall. She gazed at him and gave a little sigh, drinking in the splendour of his lean, lithe body and the perfectly shaped limbs marred only by the scars of earlier encounters with the enemy.

"You are beautiful all over," she said simply. "Come. Please, not the bed. That is for sleeping." She took him by the hand and led him across the room to where the soft rugs and cushions made a thick, luxurious pile, and they lay down together like a pair of splendid savages in a cave carpeted with fleecy hides and fur.

In the near darkness of their embrace Nick caught sight of the tiny tattooed AXE symbol on his inner elbow. It glowed faintly, a permanent and graphic reminder that he was Spy, not Savage, and the most beautiful and desirable women he had known had not always been the ones deserving of his trust. And so, even when he believed in them and loved them, he held back a fragment of his trust to stand guard and keep reminding him—along with the AXE tattoo—that he was more Killmaster than lover and that a spy had few real friends.

But it was not always easy to remember. Mirella's subtle touch electrified him. He stroked her softly and touched her in all the lovely places his eyes had shared with all those others, and then he touched the secret places that others had not seen. She trembled a little, and began the pulsating movement of her provocative dance. Only now it was real, and it found a response that gave it meaning and added vitality. Their thighs came together and rotated voluptuously until Nick's senses reeled and he felt all control slipping from him. He gently disengaged their clinging bodies and changed position so that he could start again, knowing that his every muscular movement and gently stimulating touch were giving her exquisite pleasure. And she knew the art of love as well as he; she was volatile and languorous, now lazy as a cat and then agile as an acrobat; and she gave him all the ecstatic variations her womanly knowledge and her supple body had to offer.

Sparks flew between them. They came together in a dozen different ways and lit a hundred little fires until suddenly she gasped and began to jerk beside him. He rolled over on to her and attacked as he sensed she wanted to be attacked—rhythmically, with vigour, and yet with controlled subtlety. Then she moved convulsively and held him to her and would not let him go, raising her body to bring his even closer, and he felt her tightening around him until the exquisite pleasure was too much to hold back. Wild exhilaration swept them both as one, and kept them together in their intimacy for incredibly long, impassioned moments. They parted then, first to draw breath and then to kiss, and then they made more love until the glowing embers died down to a faint, relaxing glow. Sighing, they stretched out with their bodies barely touching, and were silent.

At last she said drowsily, "I really did promise I'd go out. Do you still want to come with me? Or perhaps you have had enough of me." She eyed him pleadingly in the soft light.

Nick raised himself on one elbow and looked at her with surprise.

"Mirella! How could I have had enough of you? Of course I want to come!" He drew her to him and kissed her tenderly, feeling passion stir in him again.

She returned his kiss with something like gratitude mixed with gentle urgency, and then she pulled back with a laugh.

"No, we must not start again, or people will be bound to think it strange when we arrive together so late. But—shall we shower together?"

Nick agreed enthusiastically.

They laughed and fondled each other under the warm water like children discovering each other, and when they found the children growing up too rapidly and beginning to act like very experienced adults, they turned on the cold water and cooled off.

They both dressed rapidly, in separate rooms, and when they stepped out of her apartment they looked as cool and decorous as if they'd spent the evening discussing the respective climates of Washington and West Africa . . . both of which are very warm in summer.

THINGS THAT GO BUMP IN THE NIGHT

"No, you drive this time," he said, when she suggested that he take the wheel. "I take it that it's some distance out of town?" Mirella nodded. Nick opened the driver's door for her and helped her in. "I don't know my way around; we'll make better time if you do all the work."

He walked around the car and got in next to her, hoping that whoever might try to kill him tonight would not have done anything so nasty as mine the car to blow him up together with Mirella. The thought was not purely selfish, nor was it entirely altruistic. He sincerely hoped that she did not share his danger, and at the same time he felt that her company was something of a safeguard. Death was not of great concern to him, yet he saw no reason to be unnecessarily careless of his life—and certainly not before the job was done.

She guided the car smoothly out of the long driveway and into the broad street that led to the yet broader avenue that would take them out of town.

"You are safe with me . . ." Had she meant anything by that, beyond a reassurance that the doors were locked and no killers were lurking in the closets? Probably not. But possibly her unconscious mind had formed the words that *could* mean his life was safe as long as he was with her—and no longer than that.

They threaded their way through the late night traffic and joined the thin stream of cars heading southeast, out of the city. Mirella drove in silence and with care until she passed beyond the city limits and turned into a subsidiary route lined with tall, drooping trees that creaked with the sound of tiny frogs and hoarse-voiced birds. She slowed down to negotiate a tricky curve and let the big car pick up speed as the road straightened into a long dark ribbon.

Nick put his arm lightly on her shoulders, and she smiled.

"You haven't even asked me where we're going," she said.

"Well, we haven't had much time for idle talk. And wherever we're going, we're going. But now that you mention it—where *are* we going?"

"To a place without a name," she answered lightly, "to visit some nightbirds named Baako. I told you they are friends of Julian and Rufus? Yes, I remember that I did.

They have a small farm where I often go to—what shall I say? please do not laugh—unwind after I have been working. They let me come and go as I please, and it is most relaxing. Tonight, though, they are having a special party of some sort; I do not know what the occasion is, but they were most anxious for me to come."

"And they won't mind that you've brought a stranger with you?" Nick waited for her reaction in the dashboard light.

"Oh, no, I know they will be glad to meet you. Rufus said . . ." she stopped and sought for words.

"What did Rufus say?" Nick probed gently.

She turned a slightly embarrassed look upon him. "You understand, he mentioned you before I met you. He wanted you to meet people whom he knew would interest you, and he suggested that I take you to see the Baakos. But believe me, no matter what he said, I would have come alone tonight if I had not wanted you to be with me. And I know that you will like them."

Nick fingered her hair thoughtfully. Rufus had an interesting way of being on stage front even when he wasn't in the act.

"You do not mind?" She glanced at him anxiously.

"Of course not. How could I mind, as long as I'm with you?" His arm tigihtened about her shoulders.

They drove on in silence for some time. The road began to wind again and branch off into unpaved offshoots that led through thickening trees to what he thought must be small farmhouses.

"Ah! Nearly missed it. I do this every time." She swung the wheel suddenly and the big car skidded into a narrow, bumpy road that Nick decided must be the track to the Baako farmhouse. But it went on for several miles before she pulled up in front of a barred gate and locked the hand brake.

"Now I have bad news for you," she said apologetically. "We must go the rest of the way on foot. I should have told you before. Anyway, it is not so important if you do not mind walking a little with your evening shoes."

"My evening shoes be damned," Nick said, and kissed her. "I'll gladly walk wherever you say." Something in him ticked a warning. While there was still time, he kissed her again until his racing pulse almost drowned out the ticking. Then he stopped and looked longingly at the incredibly lovely face. "Let's go then, shall we? Walk in the woods, and meet the people, and then go home together." He smiled at her and touched her cheek. She took his hand and caressed it with her lips.

"Yes," she said softly. "Let us do that."

He helped her out of the car and she led him past a wide barred gate to another smaller one that opened easily. A moss and twig-covered path led through the overhanging trees.

"They have closed the road," she explained, "because the last rains made it almost impassable and they decided to grade it, perhaps pave it when there is time. But in the meantime the only way to the house is this path. I'm afraid it is almost a mile before we reach the house. But it is a pleasant walk, and this is a lovely night."

"It is indeed," Nick agreed. "But what do they do with their own cars?"

He felt rather than saw her sudden head movement. "Their own cars?" she repeated. "Oh, they are horsemen, all of them. There are many paths for horses through these trees."

It sounded reasonable; but his nose was sensitive and he could not smell horse along the path they walked upon. The trees were too low, anyway.

"Is this one of the bridle paths?" he asked, knowing that it couldn't be.

"Bridal . . . ? Oh, for the horses, you mean." She took his hand and laughed quietly in the darkness. "Of course not. It is easy to see that you are from the city. No, the horses cannot use this path. This is just for people."

". . . The only way to the house is this path . . ." Plus innumerable paths for horses. Was it a slip? Or just the usual imprecise way people talked? No doubt what she meant was that this was the only footpath. Which of course was what they would be expected to use.

Nick decided to be extra careful where he put his feet. As for whatever may be hidden behind the trees, he would have to rely on the darkness and those same trees to keep him from presenting too obvious a target. He jabbed the cane in front of him like a blind man. Even Mirella seemed to be having difficulty in finding her way.

"It's even darker than usual tonight," she murmured. "Because it's later, I suppose." And she squeezed his fingers lightly.

A gnarled tree loomed up squarely in their path. To the left of it was a narrow track and then another tree with sprawling roots; to its right there was a space, a clump of thick bush, then another space. Mirella paused hesitantly.

"I think it must be the centre track," she said thoughtfully. "Not that it makes much difference—they all go in the same general direction. But only one of them is the real path, and we may as well take that. Wait here for a moment." She pressed his hand. "I will take a look on this side—we should be able to see their light from here." She glided away from him in the darkness and he could hear the soft rustle of leaves and the crackle of tiny twigs beneath her feet.

Then there was silence. He waited.

After a minute her voice came back to him as clearly as if she had been standing beside him. It sounded puzzled.

"I see nothing," she called. "I cannot understand it. I *know* we should be able to see the light by now. Nicholas, you take the other path—the one to the right—while I look a little farther up this one. But don't go far, please. And talk to me, so that I don't lose you."

"All right," he said. "I'll take a look." He heard the rustle of leaves again and shuffled his feet where he stood so that she might think he was moving. "But be careful, now." And you too, Carter, he told himself.

He heard a little laugh. "Of what? We are bound to find the way before too long."

"If not," he said cheerfully, starting to follow her and leaving the other tracks severely alone, "we can always give up the whole thing and go back into town. I'm sure we'll find something to do there."

A little chuckle floated back to him, and then a gasp as her foot struck something and she stumbled. He pushed aside a low-hanging branch and saw a dim shape pitching forward and trying to regain balance by thrusting out its leg and clutching at the nearest tree. The muted rustle of twigs suddenly became a cracking, tearing sound, and even as he leapt forward to grab her falling figure she screamed "No—No—Rufus! Oh, my God! Help!" Nick's fingers had no more than touched the softness of her stockinged ankle when the ankle was gone and he was groping uselessly at the edge of a jagged pit and he heard an awful thudding sound. Mirella started screaming like a soul in hell and then the scream became an awful bubbling sound that suddenly stopped and left nothing but the rustle of leaves and the sound of falling twigs.

He fell to his knees and groped at the blackness in front of him. He knew without having to think about it that there was nothing he could do and that it was insane for him to stay in this dark, hideous place for one moment longer, but he had to see; he had to know for sure. The pencil flashlight came out of his pocket and jabbed its light into the pit below.

Mirella lay face downwards six feet below, her arms outstretched, her hands still clutching broken twigs, her thick black hair tossed to one side... But it was wrong to say that she was lying down. Her lovely, twisted body hung inches above the floor of the dreadful pit, impaled on two wickedly pointed spikes that protruded from her back. One had thrust its way through her abdomen; the other through her lungs. The pit was lined with spikes; she had needed only two.

He knew for sure. She was dead, and horribly dead. It had been quick, but she had felt it. God, how she had felt it! He doused the tiny light and heard her terrified scream echoing in his ears. Its sound was so overwhelming that he almost missed the other sound. He heard the distant rustling only when he saw the will-o'-the-wisp flicker of a light coming through the trees beyond the pit. A deep voice called out—"Mirella? Mirella?"

Nick thrust the flashlight into his pocket and pulled off his shoes. Right pocket, one; left pocket, the other. He backed silently away from the pit and melted into the cover of a tangled thicket. A second light flicked on and came slowly towards the death hole. It struck him that one animal scream was very much like another, especially from a distance. And all the flickering lights were coming from afar. Perhaps the hunters did not know which victim they had so cruelly caught. Again he waited, his mind thrusting painful questions at him. Had she known where she was leading him, and had she made a terrible mistake—for her? Or had these fiends made use of her, played some awful trick, forcing her to innocently fall into a frightful trap they'd meant for him?

The flickering lights came closer. He imagined her lovely living body in his mind and felt its passionate embrace, and a wave of agony washed over him.

"Goodbye, Mirella," he whispered to the night, and raised his cane.

The poisonous sliver flew silently through the air towards the nearest of the lights. The light arced downwards, and he heard a startled curse. A patch of blackness swayed and fell. Nick fired again. A muffled gasp. The second light blinked out.

For a few moments there was nothing but the darkness and the silence, and then the woods became alive with lights and sounds.

Nick's instinct screamed to him to run back down the path to the waiting car and get the hell away, but his mind told him to wait. He let the next light dip into the pit before he fired again, and heard an unfamiliar, grating voice cry out: "Oh! God! It is Mirella in the pit! Why do you fools lie there staring ... ?" The voice broke off, and when it came again it was a whisper packed with maniacal hatred. "The swine. The swine. The swine. Get him! You, you! To the road. He cannot be far away."

Oh, I'm not far away, Nick thought grimly, and he fired. The grating voice ended in a satisfying scream. Voices babbled, and shushed themselves, and drifted apart in the darkness carrying their small lights with them.

Nick crouched back in his thicket and followed the moving lights with his poison-dart cane as if he were a customer at a shooting gallery. Ping-pssst! Another light went out.

A machine gun chattered in the night, raking the trees

too goddamn close to where he was. He darted down the path in his stockinged feet and fired once more. No cry, no falling light. He cursed and aimed again. Pow! A yelp. Good. He moved farther down the path and brushed against a broken bough. A yell of triumph, damn their souls! and a shot ripped past his ear. The second tore through the cloth on his shoulder and left a searing pain. He ran for several zigzag yards and threw himself down flat, holding in his mind the memory of where their shots had come from.

Silence again. No flickering lights. Then footsteps crackling over twigs. He fired in their direction and enjoyed the gargling sound that followed. More rustling footsteps and a whispered consultation. His fingers itched to reach for Wilhelmina, to pump her explosive venom at them and make them feel his hatred, but he made himself sidle quietly down the rough path with his silent killer at the ready. One shot from him, and they would have him. But the stinging darts would not give him away.

Footsteps followed close behind him. He froze into the shadows and let two dark figures come towards him, jabbing their flashlights into the air for seconds and then dousing them. One, he saw, was holding the machine gun and the other a revolver. Miraculously, the stabbing flashlights missed him. The two men passed within inches and the one nearest to him brushed his sleeve and then stopped several feet away and swung around towards Nick with a whisper to his comrade. The second man turned and they both came back towards him with their weapons raised.

Nick shot at the machine gunner first and threw himself across the path. The expected scream sliced through the air... but the gun chattered and the forest path threw up little chunks of dirt over Nick's head and shoulders. He fired again, and bullets slammed into the tree behind his ear. The revolver spat. Nick aimed the dart-cane inches to the right of the spitting flame and flung himself sideways in a twisting roll. The revolver spat again even as the machine gunner moaned and dropped, and a bullet ploughed into the fleshy part of Nick's left thigh. He managed to stifle a grunt as his eyes watched the two men fall into a tangled heap and twitch together in a sort of strange love scene and then lie quiet.

He dragged himself to his feet and listened. Wind in the trees and a nightbird calling, soaring high into the air as if the world had no ceiling and the night was for beauty and love . . . Nick forced his aching body to walk quietly down the path to the tiny gate next to the big barred one. He was alone with the night and Mirella's expensive car. And he could feel the blood oozing down his shoulder and trickling down his leg.

The urge to get into that car and drive away like a bat out of hell was almost overpowering.

But Mirella was dead, and so were two four six eight God knows how many other people, and he had been seen leaving her apartment earlier in the evening, and if he went back in her car without her . . . But he was bleeding and aching in two places and it was hard enough to think, let alone to walk, and what difference did it make, anyway? He *had* been with her, Ambassador Nicholas Carter, and people—people like cops and big fat government officials—would talk and accuse and there'd be God knows what kind of international stink . . . Yeah, but she could have dropped him off before coming out here. Who was to associate him with this mess in the woods if he left the car here and—and what? And got back into town like a well-behaved Ambassador, that's what. But Christ, how? It would take hours to walk, and his leg was murder.

Nothing to it, Carter. There is no pain. Jesus loves me this I know 'cause my Yoga tells me so.

He was a mile away from the battle scene before his dazed mind stopped arguing with itself. Ambassador Carter would have to disappear, and his disappearance would look more authentic if he were *not* seen driving back into town in Mirella's big car. He walked another mile along the fringe of the narrow road before stopping to rest and listen. No sound but a quiet chirping and the faintest rustle of a breeze. No action from the Baako farmhouse, if there had ever really been a farmhouse. Nick pulled out his shirttails, tore off as wide a strip as he could without completely baring his chest, and wadded most of the cloth against his bleeding thigh. The rest he combined with his handkerchief to fashion a crude dressing for his shoulder. When he buttoned his jacket it looked almost as though nothing was amiss, except for the two holes and the two dark stains. In the dark, no one would ever notice. He hoped.

He breathed deeply before moving on. Fortunately his feet were tough from years of barefoot walking on the shale, the burning sand and pebbles of AXE'S practice grounds, and from even more years of putting his training to the test. The only thing that really bothered him was his thigh, and here the cane came in handy. His progress to the main road was rapid and almost painless, although he knew he must be losing far too much blood for a man with a walking tour ahead. Maybe, at some point he could hitch a ride . . .

A car swished past him on the highway, heading out of town. He went on walking, hugging the shadow of the trees, relying heavily on the cane but using it carefully so that he would not leave a giveaway trail of puncture marks in the earth. A truck roared by, towards the city. Ten minutes later it was followed by a car. Then nothing for a half hour.

His leg was beginning to feel the strain. Nick stopped for a few moments to draw breath and give himself a lecture on the non-existence of pain. It had taken Mirella almost an hour to drive from her place to the side road and the barred gate. That meant he had something like forty-five miles to go, or about a day's walk. Flag a passing car? *What* passing car? Anyway, that would be just as bad as roaring into town in the flashy car. He chewed over the disadvantages of a hijack, presuming anything came along to be hijacked, and discarded the idea. He started walking again. His thigh complained with every step. Three or four cars passed him during the next forty-five minutes. He ignored them all and stayed beneath the trees, walking endlessly as if on some nightmarish treadmill. And then, at last, he heard a sound he hadn't dared hope for—the slow clip-clop of horses' hooves and the creaking of cartwheels. It was coming from behind him, heading in the direction of Dakar.

He waited until he could see it coming towards him on the road. It was an open cart piled high with produce, and its driver was nodding over the reins. Surely he wouldn't mind giving a stranger a ride into town, especially if he didn't know . . .

The cane. Too bad, but it was too closely associated with Ambassador Carter to be allowed to come with him. He carefully unloaded its deadly contents and slid the darts into his wallet. Then, as the cart drew almost abreast, he scraped a groove into the earth, buried the cane and covered it with leaves. The cart had passed him. He threw himself into a loping run alongside the road and had almost made it when he saw the headlights behind him. The shadows covered him again until the big sedan had thundered by, and then he ran along the road behind the cart until he had caught it with his finger tips and could feel it pulling him. Gradually he increased his weight upon it, and when he felt completely in control of its pace and his own muscles, he pulled himself up on to it and lay flat. There had been no jolt, he knew, no sudden increase of weight to alert the driver or his horses.

Nick burrowed into the piles of bulging sacks and made himself relax. The market opened at four-thirty . . . this, fellow would be late if he didn't get cracking. As if on cue, the fellow yawned mightily and lashed out with the whip. The cart's pace increased comfortably. Nick drowsed a little, then sat up very cautiously and put on his shoes. Might as well be ready to enter the city with his boots on.

Occasional cars passed them on both sides, but if anyone saw the huddled, sack-covered form on the back of the cart, they couldn't have cared less. It was a common enough way to travel and rest, and the slightly-lightening darkness made his evening clothes look like any other set of rags.

When he saw the wattle-and-daub huts of the suburban villages gliding by on either side, he knew that he was close to journey's end.

The false dawn was already beginning to mellow the sky when the cart clip-clopped into the city's back streets and wound its way toward one of the market places. Nick stayed with it until he saw the pre-dawn traffic thickening, and slid silently off the back of the slowing cart when it turned a corner into a cobbled street. He walked several blocks towards the city centre and then slowed into a late-night stagger. Near one of the smaller hotels he flagged a sleepy taxi driver and directed him, in a drink-sodden voice, to the Hotel Majestic. The lobby was almost deserted and no one paid any attention to him when he rolled in and headed for a call box.

The Hotel Senegal took its time about answering him and putting him through to Ambassador Carter's room. Hakim finally answered in a sleepy voice. Nick chose his words carefully.

"Is your mission accomplished?"

"Indeed, yes," Hakim answered, all at once fully alert. "No visible problems. What orders?"

"It is necessary to arrange the final disappearance," said Nick. "The American is finished. Attend to the room accordingly, taking only what might be useful. Understand? There was a struggle, but he lost it. Report to me when ready, and be quick."

"Right," said Hakim. "Anything else?"

"One more thing," Nick said tiredly, feeling stabs of pain shoot through him and willing them to go away. "It is impractical for me to contact headquarters—you will soon learn what difficulties we have had tonight—and find out for me if there are any new developments. But first things first, you understand me?"

"Perfectly," answered Hakim calmly, and rang off.

Nick left the phone booth and staggered up to his room. He tended his aching body as best he could, propped chairs in front of door and windows, and fell almost instantly into a dreamless sleep.

"Lizzie Borden took an axe ... Lizzie Borden took an axe ... Lizzie Borden took an axe ..."

Nick pulled himself out of the deep well of sleep and took Wilhelmina with him to the door. A stranger stood there—a stranger with Hakim's stooped body and another face.

"For God's sake, where do you get them all?" said Nick. "Come in and take it off."

Hakim stepped in swiftly and tore off the rubbery mask

as Nick locked the door. "It has been a night to remember," Hakim said. "And in God's name, what happened to you?"

"Your report first, please," said Nick. "Sit down."

"Yes, *sir*," said Hakim, with exaggerated deference. But his strangely unmatched eyes were serious. "First, the plan went off as scheduled. Bodies moved, I checked out, came back to occupy your room, fended off attempted entries. Received your call, damaged room severely as if you had been abducted, and took all valuables. Here they are." He tossed a small bundle at Nick. "Left there, put through early call to Honest Abe. Bad news. Your friend Miss Ashton has been snatched, her living room a mess. She has been among the missing since midnight."

THE DYING IMMORTALS

It was the goddamndest, smelliest cave in all the hills of Africa. She knew it had to be, though she was no expert on the subject, because there couldn't possibly be a worse smell in all the world. It was mountain goat and monkey, dank moss as old as time and human filth almost as old, and the sickly-sweet smell of—now what the hell was it? —death, maybe, or the obscene looking root some of the old-time herbalists seemed to set so much store by.

Liz moaned and stirred. Her head throbbed like last New Year's day and her stomach churned. Cut that out, she told herself sternly, struggling against nausea and fear. Whaddya want to do—add to the mess?

The faint light of approaching dawn filtered into the cave. So at least there was fresh air somewhere near. She dragged herself into a sitting position and muttered angrily at the damp leather thongs that bound her wrists and ankles. Very clever, she thought bitterly. As they dry, they tighten. Don't take any chances, these mad bastards. Very goddamn clever...

They had come during the night when she was getting ready for bed, about half an hour before the one man

Abe had left on duty had been due to change shift and go home. She knew that he had never made it, because when she was through wrestling with the two thugs in her living room and was dragged outside, she had seen him lying outside her front door with a dagger in his back. She had yelled again and bitten hard into a fleshy hand, and then darkness had fallen like a bomb and blotted out her consciousness. After that there was a wild ride, more choked screams, more painful darkness slamming at her head.

And now this foul, filthy cave.

Come now, Elizabeth, she admonished herself. What would Aunt Abigail think, to hear you talk like that? Aunt Abigail... A sudden stab of terror shot through her. Aunt Abigail Nick Carter Abe Jefferson and Julian Makombe. They were all somehow part of this and she'd never see any of them again but what in God's name was she doing here and *where why who*?

Why was the only question that made any possible sense. Never before had she been in a spot like this, and never before had she met anyone like Ambassador Nicholas J. Huntington Carter. Trouble was his middle name, though how J. could stand for trouble was more than she could...

When she regained consciousness for the second time she felt infinitely stronger and almost able to think straight. Get out of here! she thought.

The bonds were tighter than before, and the grey-pink light showed the silhouettes of two men standing at the entrance to the cave, one looking into it and the other facing outward. And she was cold. Who wouldn't be, she thought crossly, with nothing on but panties and a bra and a bandage on the shoulder? The knowledge of her near-nakedness made her feel twice as uncomfortable but not quite twice as scared. Covered by a wave of indignation, she thought wryly; too bad it's transparent.

The sun came up more slowly than she had seen it rise over the flatness of Abimako. So I'm probably in some godforsaken valley, she thought, miles away from any hope of help. Nicholas Carter, where are you!

There were sounds of life from somewhere near. Tin

clanked against tin and a low voice hummed with early morning song. The tang of wood smoke caught at her nostrils, dimming out the other odours in her prison cave. Footsteps scrunched outside. The two guards came to attention and a third man stepped between them and entered the cave.

He walked around her, silently at first, and then he laughed.

"So the elegant Miss Ashton has come to join us in our mountain retreat," he said. "Improperly clad, I see, but no doubt feeling that anything is good enough for your inferiors. Is that it?" He laughed again. "But we must not be ungrateful. You have come here to see how the other half lives, and I will make sure that you *do* see."

His face was in darkness but his lilting voice was unmistakable.

"Rufus," said Liz. "Well, well, well. And just how do you expect me to see the sights, tied up in this foul cave of yours? And what in hell do you think you're doing?"

"Do you talk to me as your servant, Miss Ashton?" His voice was thin and dangerous. "Do you think you are in a position to take that tone with me?"

Liz sat up as straight as she could and stared at him in the gloom. "Servant"? So he was still licking those old colonial wounds...

"My tone be damned. What do you expect—thanks? You must be crazy, to do a thing like this. What's the idea?" But she knew even as she spoke that it didn't make the slightest difference what she said. The very fact of her abduction made that obvious enough, even without the bitterness of his words and the unbalance she sensed in his voice. The lilt was just a little ragged around the edges, and it rose a note or two too high. Besides that, his men had killed to bring her here. She wondered, with a chill, how many others he'd had killed. And *why*?

"The idea, Miss Ashton? You cannot guess? And I thought you were so clever!" he mocked. A knife came out from somewhere within the folds of his toga-like garment and raked down towards her, skidding to a stop in the air a bare half-inch short of her chest.

Rufus laughed softly. "You flinch, do you?"

"Naturally," she said, with icy anger. "Who wouldn't? If you want to kill me, go ahead. But don't play games with me. Just tell me why first, then get it over with. Or do you have a real reason, Rufus? Is it only spite?" She tugged at her bonds in the gloom as she spoke. Hopeless. Goddamn things were tighter than ever. Fear butterflied inside her.

"Spite?" he said thoughtfully. "No-ooo, I wouldn't say that. Not altogether. Natural hatred, one might say, of one part of the world for another. And I have no intention of killing you just yet. You see, as you continue to enjoy your stay here, I may need to offer proof that you are still alive—that is, if you are to serve your purpose. *My* purpose, I should say. And so, we will keep these in good condition, yes?" The knife jabbed lightly at her ears. "And this, and this, and these." He chuckled and probed her body with the knife point. Liz sucked in her breath. The light jabs didn't hurt but they suggested a most unpleasant future. Beads of cold sweat formed suddenly on her forehead. "You understand me now?" Rufus continued. "You are a hostage. For your friend Carter. In case my other efforts to quiet him down should come to nothing. He seems to be a very hard man to pin down. Or perhaps your experience has been otherwise? Never mind: you can tell me about that some other time." The knife snaked down between her feet, slicing carelessly through the leather thong and nipping at her flesh. "Ah! How clumsy of me. But you may as well get used to it, because if Carter does not contact my colleagues quickly—that is, supposing they have not already taken care of him—then he will have to be prodded. One or two little momentoes should do the trick, I would think, if he is anything of a gentleman. Now get up, Miss Ashton, and follow me. Up! That's it. This way, please."

He bowed with mock courtesy and waved her out of the cave. The morning glowed with a light far more cheerful than she felt was fitting, and when she looked down from the slight rise on which they stood she could see the whole sweep of the settlement he had brought her to. It was not big, but it was concentrated, a little stronghold of huts and tents virtually surrounded by low hills. An army camp, with half-uniformed muscular hulks of men attending to the morning chores. Not a very strategic position, she thought; not for defending. But what a hiding place! Especially if no one was looking for it.

"Move, please." Rufus prodded her down the slope. The two guards eyed her scanty costume with stoic indifference. Couple of queers, I'll bet, she told herself, feeling relief at their lack of interest. "Here we stop," said Rufus. "Unfortunately I must tie you up again. But you will find it warm here in the sun, and the view is good. In fact, you will find it very very warm." He tied her by the shoulders to the crossbar of an H-shaped wooden frame, facing the busiest section of the camp, and secured each leg to one of the uprights. "So, that should be sufficiently uncomfortable. Please do not concern yourself with thoughts of discomfort, heat, thirst, hunger. Think of a persuasive message to send to the prying Carter, so that he will respond while you are in reasonably good condition. And—oh, yes" He snapped his fingers. "I almost forgot, and the fat one so badly wants to know. Perhaps you will tell me who he really is?"

"Who he really *is*?" Liz stared back at him. "Why, you know as well as I do who he is. What 'fat one'? What're you talking about?"

"Ah, no. *I* ask the questions." Rufus smiled. "But I will give you time to think. Meditate, enjoy the scenery and the country air. I will come back later to continue our pleasant little chat." He inclined his head graciously and turned away, heading for the largest of the camp buildings. The little breeze that fingered his toga swirled around the camp, touched her straining body and died a sudden death. The sun burst full into the valley and rekindled the heat of yesterday.

The nearest shade tree was many yards away. There must have been a swamp or a stagnant pool nearby, because an odour of warm rot began to rise and the mosquitoes soon rose with it. They and the big bluebottle flies descened swiftly on the tempting expanse of her bare skin and began their tortuous symphony of buzzing and high whining. After a while they started biting...

Liz gritted her teeth and made herself concentrate on the scene before her. It was not a pleasing prospect. Between her and the nearest tents was a tall pole topped with an aged human skull that seemed to be staring straight down at her and sneering at her predicament. Beyond it, a little yellow man in drab uniform seemed to be lecturing a group of Nyangese tribesmen on the art of —what? Godalmighty, slitting open abdomens! His gestures were hideously graphic. In front of a low, shed-like structure another yellow man was talking quietly to a second group of avid listeners. Now what would a couple of Chinamen, Lis wondered, be doing and saying in the heart of this troubled little African nation in Rufus Makombe's cozy mountain hideaway? Unite, Coloured Nations of the World! Black and Yellow, Stick Together! Spread the Word! Kill, like this, and this and *this*!

She shuddered under the blazing heat of the sun. Kill your own brother, maybe? For an idea? Hell, no. For gain. Power. Helped on by a group of yellow men with ideas of their own. Christ, how was she going to get out of this mess and get word to Jefferson or Carter?

The mosquitoes whined and bit incessantly. The sun bore down mercilessly and the angry blotches on her body became one blazing, unbearable and sweating rash. And what exactly did Rufus expect her to do? Chew off a fingertip and send it to Nick Carter's hotel room in Dakar with her love, and would he please call upon her at his earliest convenience?

She strained against her bonds for the hundredth time. Rufus knew how to tie knots, that was for sure. Womanizing, hot-rodding, debonair younger-brother-Makombe had managed to keep a bundle of secrets hidden away beneath that handsome, carefree exterior.

Her head began to swim. She closed her eyes and tried to remember a childhood prayer. The gentle words turned into a string of curses, at herself for her helplessness and at Rufus for whatever the hell he was.

An angry, agonized bellow ripped the air. She opened her eyes to see Rufus bursting from one of the huts, his toga flapping around his ankles and his hands clenched into fists that beat furiously around him. He shouted at the groups of men as he strode towards her; the words tumbled out too quickly for her to understand, but she thought she heard a name. What was it? Mirella? Yes, that was it. Mirella . . .

Rufus advanced upon her, his face muscles working and the whites of his eyes showing huge and staring against the glossy blackness of his face.

His clenched right fist lashed out and slammed at her face.

"Killers! Killers! *Killers! All of you.*" He hit her on the other side of her face, and her head jerked painfully sideways. "Now *you* will die. Mirella—my beautiful—*my* Mirella! Why should you live when she is dead?" His fist came at her again. She ducked her head and caught the blow with her forehead. "She is dead! He killed her!" His breath came in heavy, jerking gasps, and she could see his muscles straining against the loose cloth. "Now you die, without him. Now there is no hope for you!" He kicked her brutally, like an enraged child.

"Rufus Makombe, stop!" Liz threw back her head and yelled at him. "You crawling yellow bastard, is that all the guts you have? Tie me up and make goddamn sure I don't kick you back? Get me off this thing and stop screaming like a bloody fairy!"

His fist stopped in mid-air and slowly fell to his side. She could see the yellowish-white foam that flecked the corners of his mouth. And the tears in his eyes. Rage or anguish? Both, she decided, blinking back her own.

"So you still dare to talk to me like that. And you really expect me to untie you and let you go, I suppose." The words came out of his mouth like poisoned arrowheads. "No. But you are right about one thing—it is beneath my dignity to touch you. You will die as she died." Rufus swallowed heavily and his mouth twisted into an odd, inhuman shape. "Only for you it will take longer. For you there will be suspense and fear—and then sudden death that you can see coming at you, and you will be able to do nothing but watch it and scream and take it *here*!" His voice rose to a shout and he clasped his hand to his chest like a man clutching at a knife thrust through his heart. "And then . . ." his voice dropped again, so low that it was almost a whisper, "and then your friend Carter can enjoy what's left of you before we finish *him*."

He wheeled suddenly and strode away towards the skull-topped pole, his toga flapping around his ankles and his arms outstretched like some maddened prophet of doom. He stopped suddenly, beneath the leering skull, and placed one hand on the pole as if it were a weird lance he meant to carry into battle. His other hand swept a gesture at the waiting men and his voice roared and echoed across the valley.

"My warriors—your spears!"

Liz gave a silent, hopeless cry for help. There was a swift flurry of action in front of the huts and tents, and then each man stood at attention under the burning sun with the light glinting off the razor-tips of their spears.

Rufus threw back his head and cried out: "Who is your leader?"

And the skull at the top of the pole clacked its jaws and screeched—"Rufus is your leader! Honour him—kill for him—and this land is yours! Rufus is your leader!"

Scores of voices picked up the cry and boomed it back. "Rufus is our leader!"

"What manner of men are you?" cried Rufus.

"You are invincible!" shrieked the skull. "You are invulnerable! Believe, and you will never die!"

"We will never die!" came back the chorus.

"Is your aim true?" roared Rufus. "Can you throw a ring of death around the enemy and yet let the enemy live to die a thousand deaths?"

"You will throw a ring of death," the skull said hollowly. "Rufus, your one true leader, commands it. You will throw!"

"We will throw!" the voices thundered. "The enemy will die a thousand deaths!"

"Then throw!" screamed Rufus.

"Throw, and live forever!" ordered the skull.

Feet shuffled forward and glistening arms raised their assegais in the air. The first row threw.

Liz closed her eyes.

A dozen little breaths of wind whistled past her body—over her head, between her legs, past her cheeks, skimming her shoulders . . . She opened her eyes. She was still alive. Spears were embedded all around her in the dank earth. The second row went into action and the hideous blades soared through the air to miss her by the breadth of one thin hair. A couple of them thudded into the crossbar behind her. She was a living target at a circus sideshow, a human pincushion waiting to be pricked, and she was dying a thousand deaths of agonized suspense.

The volley of spears whistled and screamed and soared and thudded and stopped; there was a ring of death around her.

The hated voice called out: "Enough of play! We will finish the woman with two more, and those two must be perfect. Who would have the honour?"

Liz opened one sweat-burned eye and waited for the clacking skull. Its jaw opened creakily. Attaboy, she thought. But Jesus God Almighty, a miracle for me too, please—don't let me die don't let me die!

"It is ordered!" shrilled the skull. "Give Rufus two good men who will not miss. Two killing spears, two men who will have eternal life!"

More spears appeared as if from nowhere and a dozen enthusiasts for eternity leapt forward. A huge man dressed in remnants of American battledress, separated himself from the horribly exhilarated crowd and bellowed like a sergeant major. The volunteers went one by one back into the ranks until only two remained, spears ready and sleek bodies taking up the throwing stance.

"One high, one low!" screamed Rufus. "Two spears for the creature in the pit! Kill, and you will live forever!"

"Kill, and live!" the skull echoed feverishly.

The first man flexed his powerful body and drew back his arm.

And suddenly his head seemed to blow off.

The second man grunted with surprise and quietly dropped.

For a moment the only sound was the echo of the shots.

And then the skull split into a hundred tiny pieces and dribbled down the pole.

Rufus stamped his feet and screamed.

An eerie voice from nowhere echoed across the valley and rolled over the stunned, disordered ranks, and shocked into silence the one man who stood and shouted his frustration to the sky.

"Are you the leader, Rufus? Are you sure that you're the leader?"

Rufus swung his head wildly, searching for the sound.

"I am the leader! I am the leader! What is this trick? Where . . . ?"

"What do you lead, Rufus? Are you the Chief of all Nyanga?"

Rufus stood stock-still for a moment. Then a smile crossed his face and he clutched his breast dramatically.

"I will be the Chief," he said proudly. "I will be King, I will be President, I will be all Nyanga!"

"Good, Rufus! Nobly said!" the voice boomed approvingly. "But what about Julian and his Russian friends? And your American enemies?"

"They are nothing!" Rufus roared triumphantly. "They will die, they will all die! I have more powerful friends, and we fight together. The gods are with me!"

"The gods and the Chinese," the voice said reverently. "Do they work together for you, Rufus? To make you the leader, Rufus?"

"They do as I tell them," Rufus shouted arrogantly. "Even the gods speak with my voice . . . " His body suddenly tightend and he looked down at the shattered skull and then at the two dead men. He looked up again and his eyes darted to the living warriors. There was silence among them but they, too, stared down at the crumpled bodies and the splintered skull; and they glanced sideways at Rufus; and they sought the source of the strange sound; then they looked back at Rufus. A low mutter ran through the tattered ranks. The two little yellow men started talking together in low, excited voices.

Rufus seemed to shrink where he stood. "Who are you?" he choked. "Come out where I can see you! Are you enemy or friend? Show yourself! Men! My warriors! Into the hills and kill!"

"No!" boomed the voice. "You will all stay where you are. I am coming down. Watch the sky behind you!"

The unidirectional microphone wavered on its slim fish-pole and withdrew.

"Behind 'em? That was a sneaky one." It was Hakim who whispered admiringly. "Here, I'll take the mike boom. Just drop the megaphone."

Nick swiftly disconnected the tiny wire recorder that was strapped to his wrist and pulled two pineapple-shaped objects out of his pocket. Behind him, Chief Abe Jefferson spoke urgently into a walkie-talkie. Several yards from him, on a high point looking straight down into the valley, Corporal Stonewall Temba adjusted his grip on the machine gun and rose from a prone position to a low crouch. Between two and three miles away, towards Abimako, a helicopter waited with its blades whirring up a wind in the hot air. And some miles behind the helicopter a line of military jeeps received a relayed message and increased its speed.

Nick rose amidst the rocks and gnarled trees of that hillside in the district called Duolo. He pulled back his arm and thrust it forward in a powerful pitching motion. The pineapple lobbed through the air. He drew back his arm again, ready for the second pitch, and watched the gratifying results of his throw. It was as if a bolt of summer lightning had struck down from the sky, and he could hear the low but startled cry of dozens of voices in the valley. *Thank you, Madame Sophia, honey,* Nick whispered fervently, watching the great fat billowing clouds swelling into the air; *thank you, for giving me the address.* He threw again.

"Let's go, Hakim. At 'em, Abe!"

They ran over the hilltop and down into the smoke-filled valley.

Liz saw the figure looming up through the thick, reddish-grey smoke and felt her heart lurch wildly. Oh, God, it's Nick, she cheered within herself. And then—Oh God! It's not! The awful shock of seeing that hideous, leering, evil face, after all the other terrible experiences, was almost too much to bear. She came close to fainting as the figure reached for her with a knife and said cheerfully: "Compose yourself. You must realize that I cannot possibly be half as evil as I look!" The awful face split into a wonderfully radiant, reassuring smile, and one firm arm held Liz while the other lashed swiftly at her bonds. "The Cavalry has come, and I am one of it!"

Several yards away the powder-bomb smoke cleared slightly and Nick appeared silently and suddenly in front of Rufus, Wilhelmina in his hand. Rufus stepped backwards with a gasp. Then he stared.

"It's Carter!" he screamed. "Kill him, kill him, kill him!"

Another voice, unknown to Nick, boomed through the drifting smoke.

"No, *you* kill him, Rufus—man who cannot die!"

DUEL IN THE SMOKE

Nick heard the low whistle that meant Hakim had freed Liz and was ready with his carbine in case things got out of hand too early. And he heard the double chirping signal that told him Abe and Stonewall had filtered down to cover the encampment with their sub-machine guns. A tall, barrel-chested figure in tattered American battledress stepped out of the smoke clouds holding up an assegai. He thrust it into Rufus' unwilling hands.

"You have lied again, Rufus Makombe," he boomed. "You make us kill and tell us that the gods protect us, that we cannot die. And still we die. Now let us see *you* kill, and live!"

Rufus backed away. "You fool! What use is this spear to me against his gun? Men! My warriors . . . !"

"Kill for yourself, or be killed, Rufus," the big voice said coldly.

Nick raised Wilhelmina pointedly.

"Who gives the orders, Rufus?" he asked softly. "You or your subordinates? I did not come to kill but to take you back with me. To your brother—the Chief of all Nyanga. Order your men to fall back."

"No!" said the big, cold voice. "He will not be taken back, white man. Fight him yourself, as man to man, or the rest of us will tear you both apart, gun or no gun. You, Rufus, *and* the woman."

"That would be a mistake," said Nick, just as coldly. "I am not alone. Abe!" He raised his voice. "Fire above their heads!"

A warning burst of fire chattered through the smoke.

The man in battledress looked calculatingly at Nick. "That makes no difference," he said softly. "It only means that many more of us will die. *Fight him!*"

Nick thought swiftly. The big man was wrong; yet he was right. That he would be able to get himself and friends safely out of that valley and far away, Nick had no doubt. But too many brainwashed, misguided men would die. And out of it all new hatred would be born.

"Then give me a spear," Nick said, and slid the Luger out of sight.

Rufus swung back his arm and threw.

Nick saw his movement as it started and ducked with time to spare. He reached behind him and pulled the still quivering assegai out of the valley floor. "In that case," he said, "give *him* a spear."

Wordlessly, the big man handed Rufus another assegai.

Rufus took it in both hands and charged. Nick crouched low and waited for him. At the last possible second he sidestepped and thrust the tip of his own spear deep into Rufus' unguarded thigh.

"Aaaarghh!" Rufus bellowed out his rage and agony and whirled on Nick like a dervish, jabbing with a lightning thrust even as he turned. The spear point ripped Nick's sleeve and bit a painful gouge into his upper arm. Nick cursed softly and leapt aside, feinting a jab at the stomach and then flipping the point of the spear upward to catch Rufus lightly in the chest as he lunged and pulled back just in time to avoid a fatal slash.

Rufus danced lightly backward, a grotesque figure in his flapping toga. Blood was seeping through the cloth that covered his thigh and his lips were drawn back from his teeth in a snarl that turned his handsome face into an ugly mask. The toga put him at something of a disadvantage, but he seemed to be gaining confidence and speed. Nick's assegai flashed. Rufus parried expertly, came in quickly with a light stabbing motion that pricked at Nick's left side, and danced away. Nick heard an "Aaahh!" of approval coming from somewhere in the smoke. He knew that his own performance was nothing to "Aaahh" about; the two bullet creases of last night had so stiffened both his leg and shoulder that his footwork and his thrust were far short of their usual skill. He decided on a change of tactic.

Rufus bent low, held his assegai like a lance, and charged.

Nick dropped before him like a stone. Almost instantly, he came to life again, jerking his body upward beneath Rufus' flying, stumbling legs, and felt his enemy leap frogging clumsily over him. He made a leaping turn with his spear held in front of him across his body, his hands spread wide apart along the shaft, and watched Rufus hit the dirt.

"Up, Rufus!" he called invitingly. "Stand up and come and get me."

Rufus sucked in the dusty air and grabbed his fallen spear. He was breathing heavily when he came at Nick, and his movement was no longer swift and sure. Nick pivoted and swung his weapon like a stave—the Japanese stave called the *bo*, which does nothing so crude as lunge or club but twirls like a drum majorette's baton. It twirled now, describing an invisible, perfect circle that was marred only by contact with Rufus' spear. There was a sharp clack of wood against wood. Rufus came to a blundering, startled stop, his hands empty and his eyes searching wildly for his lost spear. Nick heard it clatter to earth yards away. Deliberately, he threw his own spear to the ground. Rufus growled like a wounded animal and darted for it with his hand outstretched. Nick leapt and grabbed Rufus' hands in his now sinewy clutch, jerked him close so that the dark sweating face almost touched his, and ground a series of twisting jabs into the breast plate and heart. Rufus groaned and grunted and struggled feebly. Nick gave it to him with a right fist-hammer to the heart that held back nothing. Something cracked sickeningly. Rufus' face and body twisted with the awful agony. His eyes glazed; and he dropped.

Nick drew a couple of slow, deep breaths and pulled out Wilhelmina. He heard a low groan rising from the valley. He looked about him for the first time in many minutes and saw that most of the thick smoke had lifted. Abe and Stonewall had stationed themselves at strategic positions near the huts but still high enough up the slope to command the whole encampment. Hakim, now without his bush shirt, was stationed only feet away from Nick's left shoulder, his carbine raised in readiness and aiming steadily at the big man in the ragged battledress.

The big man stepped forward uncertainly.

"Is he dead?" he asked, and his voice was a cracked half-whisper.

"What difference does it make?" Nick answered quietly. "He's finished. See for yourself if he's dead—if you think it matters. And the rest of you can fight and die for nothing, if you want to. Or you can stop working for your enemies and start thinking for yourselves. You'll be under arrest within the next few minutes whatever you decide. So take your choice. Die for the yellow men; live to make something of your country." He stopped suddenly, full of things he wanted to say but not knowing how to say them. Anyway, it was a pretty ridiculous thing for a counterspy called Killmaster to do—lecture about the dangers of foreign intervention and the joys of national pride. "It's up to you," he finished abruptly, and turned on his heel.

The brisk, chopping sounds of helicopter blades filled the valley. Nick heard Abe Jefferson's crisp voice bark out an order.

"Where's Liz?" he asked Hakim.

Hakim winked horribly. "Behind the tall rocks, there, beautifying herself for you and scratching mightily. Be careful—she has my .22 and an itchy trigger finger. Plus itchy almost everything."

Nick strode through the wispy smoke and found her, draped in Hakim's bush jacket and hastily pulling a man's short comb through her tangled hair and waving the pistol like a can of insect spray.

"Liz! You all right?" he asked anxiously.

"Oh, *wonderful*!" she said enthusiastically. "Thanks just a heap. It's been the *greatest*, the whole thing." She dropped the comb and gun and fell into his arms.

It was only moments later that the valley began to fill with smartly uniformed men. Nick led Liz to the waiting helicopter. Hakim followed, leaving Abe and Stonewall with the joint team of army and police.

There was plenty to talk about on the smooth flight back to Abimako. But there were two questions, and one fascinating answer, that hung in Nick's mind for a long time afterwards.

The first came from Liz. Her question cut abruptly into one of those sudden silences that break up intense conversations.

Liz looked up from her survey of the African plains below and said: "Who was Mirella?"

"I'm not quite sure," Nick answered slowly. "And I don't think I'll ever really know."

The second came from Nick himself.

"By the way," he said to Hakim, "just what was it you said you teach at the University? The Seven Lively Arts?"

"That's right." Hakim grinned cheerfully. "Ambush, Burglary, Disguises, Mugging, Stabbing, Strangling, and Diversionary Tactics. Other elements, too, of course, but those are basic. Please, Miss Ashton! I assure you I am harmless. It is seldom I get the opportunity to practise what I preach." He managed to focus both eyes on Nick's startled face. "I am a criminologist," he said. "It has long been my belief that the only way to beat the criminal at his own game is to know his every trick."

"And you know them," Nick said, almost reverently. "Man, you really know them!" He threw back his head and laughed with pure delight.

And even while he laughed he thought: AXE could use a man like this. I'll talk to Hawk.

Julian Makombe stared at them from the pillows of his hospital bed. His face was drawn but his eyes were alert—and filled with horrified disbelief. He looked from Nick to Liz to the stranger called Hakim and to his wiry, trusted Chief of Police.

"I cannot believe it!" he said. "It can't be true! My brother Rufus and the Red Chinese! You have made this up, you must have. He has never—and I know this, because he is my brother—I *know* he has no interest in politics or power. Jefferson, what is this madness?"

Nick touched a switch on the tiny wire recorder. "I would not have believed it either," he said quietly, "of my own brother, or yours."

The small machine hummed softly. An eerie voice floated across the hopital room.

"Are you the leader, Rufus? Are you sure that you're the leader?"

"I am the leader!" Rufus yelled metallically. *"I am the leader!"*

Julian drew in his breath in a choking gasp, and listened.

I will be President, I will be all Nyanga ... Julian and his Russian friends ... They are nothing—they will die ... I have more powerful friends ... The gods and the Chinese ... They do as I tell them ...

The damning words washed over him. Nick watched and pitied, and clicked off the recorder.

"Is it all true, then?" Julian whispered. "Abe—Chief Jefferson—is it true?"

Abe nodded soberly. "I saw it all. I heard it. Mr. President, it's true. I am sorry."

Julian sighed. He turned his gaze to Nick "And so you killed him," he said flatly. His tired eyes flickered over to Liz. "I cannot forgive him for what he has done—to all of us. To all of you. But I wish ... I wish that I could have spoken to him."

"You will be able to," Abe said briskly "You will be well long before he is, but he is far from dead. Merely incapacitated. He'll live."

Julian achieved one of those curious reversals common to those weakened by illness. He turned his head to Nick and said: "He would be better dead. You should have killed him."

Nick rose from the bedside.

"Perhaps," he said quietly. "But I could not bring myself to kill the brother of the man who asked me here to help him."

Julian stared at him. Something of the shadow lifted

from his gaunt face. "I expected an unorthodox ambassador," he said, "but nothing quite so extraordinary." He sighed, and then the suggestion of a smile touched his lips. "I hear you disappeared from your hotel room in Dakar?"

"I did," said Nick. "Ambassador Carter came to an inexplicable end. I don't know what Dakar is coming to."

"Neither do I," Julian answered gravely. "But you can be sure that I'll send my condolences and thanks to your State Department."

They left him, then; left him to the nurses and the doctors and his thoughts.

The immensely fat man sat behind the desk and stared across it. Disgust and loathing exuded from his yellow, moon-shaped face as the sibilant voice snaked about his ears.

"I wasss unfortunate," said the other man, in his peculiarly nasal tone that was half-whine, half-hiss. "The first time I wasss naturally interesssted in the other man, that ssskulking Arab . . ."

"I already know about the first time," snapped the fat man. "What about Dakar—what went wrong there?"

The man with the green face shrugged and stuck out his lower lip.

"What could I do? My arrangementsss were already made, to have that Carter brought to me and questioned, but Rufusss wasss determined to have him killed at once —all he wanted to do was get rid of him and not bother about finding out how much he knew or who elssse he might be working with."

"What happened in Dakar?"

"I am *telling* you. We *agreed* that I was first to try to force the American to talk, but Rufus kept getting in the way. He *would* keep sending his killers after Carter, and alerting him so that he became ten times more cautious than he was before. It made things most *difficult* for me." The whining voice was querulous. "It was hard enough—as it was."

"And the Hop Club? How did you miss him there?" The fat man shifted impatiently in his gigantic chair. The rolls of fat that reached from his shoulders to his ears bobbled like agitated jelly. "Come, Laszlo, you have not done well. Explain how you failed the second time."

"How could I know it was him?" Laszlo hissed indignantly. "He came disguised as a drug peddler from here, from Casablanca. I did not even know who he was when I went after him, and then he shot me in the ssshoulder, the ssswine! *After* that, *bleeding* as I was, I got the ssstory from that fat—that is to say, from Madame Sophia. She had even mentioned the Big One in Casablanca, the ssstupid old drab! And when she saw our radio operator was dead, *and* the police came pounding at the front door, she got frightened and threatened to tell some wild story that would save her neck and hang the rest of us, give away our entire operation. So of course I had to kill her, and I jussst barely managed to get away before the police came through to the back." His frog-lidded eyes drew together in a frown as he recalled his narrow escape. Then they brightened suddenly. "You may care to know how I managed with Madame Sophia, whom as you know is of a size considerable compared with me. I selected the stabbing knife, the one with the long blade, and positioned it—thus!" He shot his right cuff and a gleaming spike appeared in his hand. "Then I jabbed at the soft underbelly . . . !"

"Enough!" The fat man shuddered tremendously. "Spare me these frightful details. I do not care to hear of your atrocities. What became of the man Carter?"

"But surely you will be interested in the finesse of my deed."

"Silence!" The big moonface twisted with distaste and anger. "And do not try to tell me how bravely you suffered with your miserable shoulder. I want to know what further attempt you made to find Carter, and what happened to him."

Laszlo's sickly face looked hurt and sullen.

"He's disappeared. There were radio reports that he had been abducted from his hotel room. I naturally assumed that Rufus' men had found him."

"Well, your natural assumption was wrong!" the fat man barked. "Or do you think it was his ghost who showed up in Duolo and took over the camp? And killed

Rufus, or whatever he did to him? Can you explain why we have heard nothing from our own sources in Nyanga since your idiotic, fright-born killings in the herbalist's shop and your equally idiotic flight to Dakar? No? I thought not! Stop trembling like a cowardly fool and put your sodden mind to work."

The froggy eyes were glazed and the slim, killer's hands were shaking. "Rufus dead?" Laszlo whispered. "Then who will take Nyanga for us?"

"Rufus is nothing," growled the fat man. "We will find another Rufus—in Nyanga, or some other country. He is not important. Unless . . ." He leaned forward and stared piercingly at Laszlo. "Unless your careless tongue has slipped and you have told him where our headquarters are. Because if you have, and if he *is* still alive, then our entire African operation falls apart. And I will take *you* apart with my own bare hands." The menace of his big, slightly sing-song voice lashed across the room.

"No-no-no!" Laszlo babbled. "I told him nothing, you must know that. I have always talked about you as if your orders come directly from Peking. He thinks you went back there after giving him the money and technicians. I was always careful to relay your messages as though . . ."

"You had better be right, Laszlo. You had better be. You have made enough mistakes. And one of them was to let Carter get as far as the Hop Club. There is one way to redeem yourself, and one way only."

"Yes-yes? Yes?" Laszlo darted his head like a snake and waited eagerly.

"Find Carter," the mountainous man said icily. "Find him quickly and bring him here to me."

"But *how* can I find him?" Laszlo hissed desperately. "As far as I know, he has disappeared. He may be dead; he may have left the country."

"You are a fool. He is not dead, and I can guarantee that he has not left Africa without trying to find out who was backing Rufus." He frowned suddenly. "I can only hope that Teng and Chan had the grace to kill themselves before anyone could question them. They must have been seen in that mountain camp . . . But they are soldiers.

They know what to do. Not like you, you miserable worm!" He banged his huge fist on the desk in a burst of rage. Laszlo flinched. "You! *You* have done nothing right. Find Carter, and I may—I *may*—decide not to punish you as I would like to. Don't ask me where to find him—that is your problem. You can be sure he is no longer in Dakar. And there is nothing left for him to do in Nyanga, thanks largely to your bungling." His thick voice was bitter and his huge face was a gargoyle mask of loathing. "So your task should be easy."

Laszlo swallowed and his body shook. "But where?" he whimpered. "How?"

The vast fist slammed down again on the immense desk top. The fat man rose abruptly and the huge chair fell back behind him.

"I told you not to ask me that!" he roared. "But I will tell you, since that prying, spying creature must be found or he will ruin us! Show yourself. Make yourself public, as you have so successfully done before. Make him find you; he will want to find you. Dangle yourself like bait in front of him. Lure the shark. Where? you ask? Where?" The fat man's face darkened into purple. "Where else but Casablanca? Don't you think that you have let him find out enough by now so that he will come straight to Casablanca?"

The stubble-faced seaman who sat at the waterfront bar looked nothing at all like Nick Carter except for the muscular toughness of his body, and he was beginning to feel less like him as the hours and days went by. "Our man in Morocco" had been a mine of information about smuggling and narcotics and had offered a long list of places frequented by people specializing in either one. He had also provided the names of several brokers, importers and small shipping companies who seemed to prefer dealing with the East rather than the West, and Nick had painstakingly enquired into every one of them. But so far the score was zero.

He ordered another beer and decided for the hundredth time that his best bet was to keep haunting the dives and the back streets in the hope of making contact with someone who would talk too much, try to sell him something, maybe lead him where the action was. It was a long shot, but not as long a shot as his even greater hope—that somewhere in these sinks and dens and flophouses he would catch sight of Green Face.

His eyes roamed casually around the noisy, smoke-filled barroom. There wasn't a single customer in it that he would trust within reaching distance of his pocket, but neither was there one—not only here, but in any of the other dives—that he could remotely associate with Green Face or dope traffic or a mystery man known to him only as the Big One or the Fat One.

He and Liz had come to Casablanca the day after the meeting in Julian's hospital room. With Abe, he had spent the remainder of the long day in fruitless questioning and investigation into the nature of the Red Chinese operations in Nyanga, and the whereabouts of Green Face and the Fat One. The day ended, as all good days should, in bed. After a while Nick and Liz had emerged from their haze of happiness, and she had asked him then if she could come with him to Casablanca.

"You're a sucker for punishment, aren't you?" he said admiringly. "Don't you realize it could be dangerous? No, Liz, you'd better not come."

"What can happen?" she murmured, brushing his ear with her lips. "I'll stay quietly in the background. Anyway, after Duolo, I can put up with anything!"

He felt her large, firm, luscious breasts against his body and gave in without a struggle. But he did insist that they stay at separate hotels—he in a dump to suit his disguise and she in the comfortable *Transatlantique*—and arrange to meet with the greatest of caution.

And so she was window-shopping and taking sightseeing tours from her hotel while Nick prowled the seamier parts of the city in his search for Green Face.

Two men who had been huddled at a corner table talking in low whispers got up and made their way—looking secretive and conspiratorial—out of the dingy bar. Nick suddenly decided to follow them. What the hell, he wasn't accomplishing anything here, and they might just lead him some place he hadn't thought of going.

They did. He followed them for several blocks before they scuttled furtively into a shambling house Nick knew—by hearsay—to be the local brothel. He gave up in disgust and headed slowly for his own hotel, intending to call Liz. But his route led past the *Transatlantique*, and he glanced automatically at its lobby doors as he passed. Several people were going in. And there was something very familiar about the back of one of them. Nick stopped and stared.

He'd have known that figure anywhere.

IN A MOORISH GARDEN

GREEN FACE! At last! But what in hell was he doing going into the hotel where Liz was staying?

Nick crossed the street against the blaring of the traffic and raced into the lobby. With his grimy seaman's clothes and his three-day beard, he was hardly the sort of guest to be welcomed by the Hotel *Transatlantique*. But the doorman merely eyed him in passing as someone to be gotten rid of it he made a pest of himself, but let him enter the hotel unchallenged.

Green Face stood at the Enquiries Desk waiting for attention. Nick sidled up behind him and waited for the clerk to notice the unpleasant little man with the anxious look in his strange, staring eyes. Nick heard him say: "I am looking for a friend of mine who neglected to tell me where he would be staying when he came to town. Is Mr. Nicholas Carter registered here? Or does he have a reservation?" The clerk consulted something. "No, sir," he said finally. "We have no record of him." "Are you sure?" Laszlo persisted. "He isss a very important American diplomat and may be travelling incognito. A tall man, youngish, carrying a cane..." "No, sir!" the clerk said firmly. "No American gentlemen. No one like that."

The man called Laszlo turned away, the very picture of despondence. Nick moved off and pretended to study the glass-encased hotel directory, keeping one sharp eye on

Laszlo. All at once the man stiffened and sucked in his breath, Nick following his gaze. Liz was stepping out of the express elevator, looking—as usual—slightly larger than life-size and twice as fresh and lovely as any woman within miles. She made her way, with graceful majesty, toward the lobby doors, unaware that every male eye was upon her and completely unconscious of the particularly interested stare of two very special pairs of eyes.

Laszlo smiled to himself and strolled after her.

And Nick strolled after *him*—relieved, perturbed, amused, thinking of the way he and Hakim had foxed and followed this little man that day in Abimako.

He let Green Face follow Liz through the main shopping centre and linger half a block away from her as she stopped outside a lingerie shop and looked into the window. Then he made his first move. He walked past Green Face and shambled up to Liz.

"Buy you a drink, lady? You come with me, I'll give you a good time." Liz turned around as if slapped and stared at him with disgust.

"That's right, look mad, and stalk away," Nick whispered urgently. "Go straight back to your hotel and stay there 'til you hear from me. Green Face is following you. Now go."

Comprehension flooded into her eyes. "Why you cheap masher!" she said through her teeth. "I'd know you anywhere. Good luck—get him!" Liz drew herself up haughtily and stalked away, back to the hotel. Nick said a dirty word and spat on to the pavement. Green Face waited for Liz to go by and then followed her casually as a man with nothing in the world to do but stroll the sidewalks of sunny Casablanca.

Once inside the lobby he was not so casual. Nick saw him pause in front of the Enquiries Desk and then move away uncertainly, as if he did not know what question he could ask. Liz was out of sight.

Maybe, Nick thought hopefully, he doesn't know her name. And why should he? She's just someone he's seen around Abimako; there's no reason why he should know the names on the American Embassy list.

Green Face sat down near the elevators and waited.

So he *didn't* know who to ask for.

Nick ignored the disapproving glance of the girl at the newsstand and bought a newspaper. He sat down near Green Face and hid his grimy face behind the paper, hoping that Green Face would make his move before the house dick was called to remove that dirty seaman from the *Transatlantique's* nice lobby.

The house dick must have been busy with other things. Green Face sat and sat. Nick waited. No one seemed to notice either of them. Time ticked by. Mid-afternoon turned to late afternoon; late afternoon to nightfall. Liz was probably bored stiff and wondering what in hell was going on. It was funny, though, Nick grinned to himself. Laszlo had apparently been looking for him in the better part of town where diplomats are supposed to stay, and he had looked for Laszlo where he knew the runt really belonged.

Laszlo started looking at his watch. Finally he got up and made a phone call from a public booth. When he came out he was shaking. He stood outside the booth for a moment staring into space; then he walked through the lobby as if he scarcely knew where he was going and started pacing back and forth on the sidewalk like a man torn between duty and some urgent personal need.

Nick watched him curiously, noting the staring eyes and the clumsy, jerking movements. Why, the bastard needs a fix! he thought. And maybe I can give it to him.

Laszlo must have come to some sudden decision. All at once he started walking rapidly away from the hotel, past the bright lights and the white buildings that gleamed under the lamps. He headed toward the waterfront and a dockside taxi stand.

Nick didn't care too much for the follow-that-cab routine in a city and among people he was not particularly familiar with. All it needed was one cab-driver to say "Huh?" in Arabic, and he had had it. Wilhelmina slid easily into his hand as his pace quickened behind Laszlo.

"Greeting, friend!" he said cheerfully, jabbing the Luger into the smaller man's back and feeling it go rigid. "Don't turn suddenly and don't shout. Understand? Keep your hands away from your body and turn and face me in a nice, friendly way."

Green Face turned slowly and stared at Nick. His face looked as though it had been dipped in olive oil and his body seemed to be squirming within its clothes, but the eyes still had their weird effect on Nick. He felt his flesh creep, as though a thousand tiny, slimy snakes were slithering over him. Then Green Face gasped with recognition, and the feeling went away.

"Now we will find ourselves another taxicab," said Nick, "and you will take me to the fat man."

Conflicting expressions chased themselves across the other man's face. "What fat man?" he said, and his trembling right hand steadied itself momentarily before making a small, convulsive movement. The long stabbing blade flashed into his hand as if by magic. But there was nothing wrong with Nick's reflexes after several days of comparative rest. His left leg swung upward in a thunderbolt of a place-kick and the knife flew skyward and arched gracefully through the air, disappearing into the gloom beyond the lamp-posts.

"That was foolish," Nick reproved him. "You know your boss would like to talk to me as much as I would like to talk to him. Don't try that again. But just in case you get any ideas . . ." His left hand shot out in a movement twice as rapid as Laszlo's drawing of the knife and clamped a deceptively light hold on the throwing arm—then made a wrenching, whiplash movement that tore a choked scream from Laszlo's throat and made him clutch his arm as though it would fall off. He swore terribly.

"Be quiet," Nick ordered. "Unless you'd like the same treatment for the other arm. Now move. We'll take a taxicab *I* will choose and you will give the directions." He prodded the cursing, hissing Laszlo with Wilhelmina's cold, unfriendly nose, and steered him into a brightly-lit street where he flagged a cruising cab.

"Tell him," said Nick. "And tell him right. If we don't find the place within half an hour I'll stop the cab wherever we are and deal with you."

"But it might—it might take longer than that," stammered Laszlo.

"It better not," Nick said grimly.

Laszlo gritted his teeth and gave the driver an address unfamiliar to Nick, consisting of two street names he had never heard of. Arabic names.

"Now tell him not to stop right outside when we get there but to drive past—while you point out the place to me—until I tell him to stop."

Laszlo, breathing heavily and trembling like a man with the ague, passed on the instructions in stumbling Arabic not much better than Nick's own and subsided into the corner.

The cab sped past the bright lights and skyscrapers of the modern city and skirted the edges of the new Medina—the new "old" section, built in Moorish style—and then slowed down to pick its way into the old Arab town with the square white buildings and ornate wrought-iron gates. After about twenty minutes Laszlo sat up straight and began to dart anxious looks out of the window. A little while later the cab turned into a wide street lined with three- and four-storied dwelling houses that reminded Nick of brownstones, except that they were a flaky white and the roofs were of uneven height. The driver braked.

"Go on to the next block," Nick ordered. "Which is it, Laszlo?"

Green Face shivered and pointed. "Third from the end. Ten Wong, Rare Books."

"Odd place for a shop," said Nick. "I don't see any sign."

"Very exclusive place," said Laszlo. "Ten sees only the wholesale dealers. He does not like the busy streets of town. For God's sake, let us stop now!"

"All right," Nick said agreeably. "Let's go and give Ten Wong a nice surprise. Have the driver pull up and pay him off."

Laszlo glared. "*I* should pay him?"

"Come on, pal. Step on it. Unless you'd like us to drive around all night and talk?"

Laszlo moaned, hissed irritably at the driver and paid him.

Nick let the cab drive off before starting back towards the Moorish house of Ten Wong, dealer in rare books.

Laszlo scuttled in front of him, his movements convulsive and his breath coming in short gasps.

"Not so fast," Nick cautioned. "We want to make a dignified—and *quiet*—entrance. Now tell me this: How many people are in that house?'"

"One only," Green Face panted. "Ten Wong himself."

"You're lying," Nick said coldly. "You want to take a nice long walk and tell me the truth? *How many people are there in that house?*" He prodded Laszlo to a stop and jabbed him with Wilhelmina.

"It is the truth!" gasped Laszlo, his face muscles twitching with his need and pain. "We must go on! I do not lie—there is only Ten himself. People come and go, but there is no one else there tonight nor all this week. The place is like a fortress—he needs no bodyguard, if that is what you're thinking of."

"A fortress, huh? But you'll get me in, won't you?" Laszlo nodded feverishly. "And who are all these people who come and go?"

"Buyers," Laszlo whined. "Clients. Customers."

"Buyers of what?" Nick insisted. "And don't tell me books."

"Yes, books!" Laszlo hissed. "The new Koran, textbooks, instruction books, all kinds of books!"

"Not so loud, you idiot. You still want to take that walk?"

Laszlo gibbered into silence.

"Now. What do the people want with Ten?"

But Green Face opened and shut his mouth wordlessly and stared wildly around for an avenue of escape. Nick realized that if he pushed the man any further he was likely to push him beyond all possible use.

"All right," he growled. "Move along. And be quiet about it."

They crept quietly through the night and stopped at Ten Wong's house. The door was a solid arch-form of oak and brass set into a whitewall archway.

"There is a signal,'" Laszlo muttered, jerking like a puppet.

"That's too bad," said Nick. "Get in without the signal or we'll walk around until you do."

Laszlo groaned and reached into his pocket.

"Be careful what you take out of there," Nick warned.

A bunch of keys came out. Laszlo move one inside the lock until something clicked, and then another inside the same lock until there was another click. He pushed lightly with his twitching fingers and the door swung open. Nick shoved him through the open door and pushed it shut behind him, noting that they were in a square courtyard with the dim sky above and thinking that Laszlo had served his purpose and now it was time to—

Laszlo pivoted with startling swiftness and raised his left arm to thrust it against the wall next to the door, muttering something indistinguishable about "the switch." Nick leapt at him and spun him sideways, bringing up Wilhelmina's butt even while he spun and slamming it down towards Laszlo's glistening temple. It was not his most effective blow; Laszlo squirmed with the agility of desperation and caught the gun butt on the shoulder Nick had wounded in Dakar, and he screamed piercingly into the night. Nick swore beneath his breath and hit him again, Laszlo crumpled and fell. And as he fell something long and snakelike caught him about the neck, dragged him for a foot or two into the courtyard, and whipped him high into the air. What the hell! Nick had time to think to himself, as he cast a swift, incredulous glance around the luxuriantly plant-filled courtyard, dimly beautiful under the soft starlight but mostly shadowed by the four high walls around it. Then a groping tendril of something that smelled like jungle undergrowth wrapped itself tightly around his gun arm and tugged.

Nick gasped and tugged back. A whiplash movement came from somewhere and a leathery thong shot around his waist, sweeping him off his feet and hoisting him aloft to dangle him high above the ground. The goddamn *plants!* Every hideous one of them—and they crammed the entire courtyard but for a narrow path from the garden doorway to another brass-bound door opposite—swayed and waved in an awful ballet of death, some of them little more than inches high and others ten, twelve, fourteen feet tall and ghastly with menace. Immense leaves, he saw, were folding over the unconscious—maybe dead—Laszlo, and the tendrils that had swept the twitching hophead into the frightful garden had released him and were waving free above his head as if in triumph.

Nick struggled frantically within the boa constrictor-like grasp. His right hand still held Wilhelmina though his arm was caught, but she was useless to him in a spot like this. He found Hugo with his left hand and jabbed feverishly at the tightening band around the waist. The things that held him in their strangle-grip reared like startled horses and writhed painfully but still held on. Hugo slashed and sliced. One of the tendrils fell away and another instantly took its place, tightening excruciatingly about his waist. Nick stabbed at it and it seemed to flinch but squeezed him even tighter. It was impossible to stab at all these reaching, twining, clinging things. The only advantage of the slashing knife was that it seemed to produce a sort of reflex action—that mane-tossing motion that swung him for moments as if on a trapeze.

And maybe he could use the motion. Laszlo had tried to say something about a signal and a switch, and then he had reached for the courtyard wall, beside the door. Something had to control these things. They were live, all right, but still they had to be controlled. Maybe there was a sound inaudible to him that made them writhe and sway this way, or maybe some kind of black light or invisible ray that kept them in this horribly agitated state as guardians of the courtyard door. Anyway, there *had* to be some way of deactivating the loathsome things; Laszlo had obviously known about this vile trap and had tried to save himself by reaching for... something.. on... that wall. Nick stabbed again and forced a clutching tendril to let him turn his head. In the dim light, through the great pod-like leaves, the twisting tendrils and the weirdly writhing shadows, he could see a small switch on the wall—something like a bell-button, or an elevator switch. That could be it. Maybe the whole damn place would flood with light if he could reach that thing and push it, but that was a chance he'd have to take.

He stabbed with renewed determination and swung his body mightily as he felt the trapeze-like swaying motion begin. Stab and swing... stab and swing... stab and swing... It seemed to him that he was gathering momentum and gaining distance, like a child pushing himself higher and faster on a playground swing. He urged his body on to even greater efforts and thought he could feel the tendrils straining and sending out reinforcements to hold on to him. Laszlo was completely out of sight—as if he mattered any longer. Nick swung. Close. Closer, closer, damn you, Carter! His foot missed by inches. Stab, swing, kick. Stab, swing. kick.

The kick connected.

Nick felt rather than heard the slight click of the pushbutton as it snapped into the wall and snapped back out again. One-button dual switch, he thought, swinging back and stabbing still. Whatever it does, the one button can be switched both on and off.

It didn't seem to do anything. No lights came on; no sounds either stopped or started. But there was an indefinable change in the atmosphere. Almost imperceptibly, the constricting clutch around his arm and waist seemed to be loosening. And then the thing that had been trying to twine itself around his neck drooped like a dying fern and lost all interest in him. The thick tendril around his waist flinched as usual as he slashed at it but its tossing reflex opened. Nick dropped lightly to the ground. His eyes raked the courtyard and the house as he struggled to catch his breath. One door at the opposite end of the narrow pathway, flanked by two heavily barred windows. One door behind him. Two completely blank walls—no, not completely blank; hard to spot at first beyond this mass of murderous jungle plant, but there it was—a stairway to the roof. A dim light went on behind one of the barred windows. Nick raced for the stairway and had reached the last step when a brilliant floodlight filled the courtyard.

He threw himself down and peered cautiously over the edge of the roof and gasped at what he saw under that bright white light. The tall, dreadful plants were swaying feebly and their great leaves were opening and closing like hands clapping very, very slowly. Then they stayed open, and the writhing stopped. Laszlo hung suspended for a moment, cupped in one of them like an ugly baby in some nightmarish treetop cradle, his eyes wide and staring in a face that was even greener than ever. Then he slid very slowly from the unfolding leaf and thudded to the ground.

There was silence and stillness for a long moment. Then the great brassbound door into the house opened slowly. Something moved very cautiously inside, and waited, and waited, and moved again.

A huge man stood in the doorway staring out into his floodlit horror garden; an immense, gargantuan obscenity, a mountain of bulging, rolling flesh that made Madame Sophia positively sylphlike by comparison. He held a long-barrelled gun that Nick knew to be as powerful and lethal as they come, but it looked like a ridiculous matchstick toy against that vast bulk of wallowing fat.

The man stepped ponderously on to the path and looked across at the prone figure lying beneath the limp and listless plants.

"Laszlo!" he said, and his tone was all disgust and loathing. "You blundering fool!" The man-mountain moved closer to the fallen figure. "So you managed to turn it off, eh, you moron?" One shapeless leg swung at the body and landed with a thump. "Get up, you..." Suddenly the fat man became a monument in stone. Only his eyes moved. They stared down at Laszlo's dead face and at the broken bits of plants left lying there by the lashing Hugo, and then he turned very slowly back towards the open door of his house.

Nick knew that once the fat man had closed that great brass-and-oak door behind him, his own chances of ever getting into the heavily barred house were very slim indeed. He raised Wilhelmina. But, slowly and carefully as the fat man was moving and as huge a target as he was, the angle was awkward and the thick growth—which he seemed to be hugging for cover as closely as he could—obscured him. Nick fired. But not at the fat man.

He fired at the single switch with the dual purpose, and even AXE's F.B.I. Instructor would have grudgingly admitted that the shot was good. It slammed into the switch. Somewhere below him Nick heard a startled gasp and partly saw the immense body turn and search around for the marksman. He decided to be helpful, and sent two shots pounding into the doorway. That should make him hesitate before he cuts and runs, Nick thought grimly. If he *can* run.

This time he was aware of the plants beginning to react. There was still no change in light or sound, but the faintest of vibrations came to him from below. He still did not know what caused it, but it scarcely mattered. The tendrils started waving. Nick fired three slow-paced, well-placed shots at the front door to serve as a distraction, and saw the big leaves start to open and shut, again like vast hands slowly clapping. And then the fat man squealed: a rat caught in his own trap. The plants were suddenly very, very busy. There was no scream, but there was a series of grunts and strangled gargles and a vast threshing about. The strange garden went wild with darting, writhing, clasping, clapping movements, and the sounds grew more frantic—big sounds, heavy sounds, muted sounds, urgent sounds, like a couple of elephants copulating.

It seemed to take ages. But then the man was so obscenely huge. Slowly, the monstrous plants tugged and twined and choked . . . then the gurgling screams began. The sighing, rustling noises drowned them out.

At last, when it was all over, Nick crossed the roofs of the adjoining houses and lowered himself to the street. His part of the job was done. Now he just had to make sure that no innocent from the outside world wandered into that hell garden, and to have the place thoroughly searched. He locked the courtyard door from the outside with his own Lockpicker's Special, and then fled through the eerie night to make contact with our Man in Morocco. Then he would call Liz.

Casablanca Airport on a day of farewells can be as miserable a place as any in the world. Today its roaring, humming sounds were blue notes of departure, half-tones speaking of business that only seemed unfinished because it was all over, except for the last goodbyes.

The fat man's frightful garden had succumbed—writhing horribly—to flame-throwers, and his house had yielded its secrets. Books, mostly; Laszlo had been almost right. Textbooks on the training of guerrillas and the use of superstitions; copies of the Koran, as rewritten by the Communists; plans for agricultural stations to be staffed by Chinese instructors; manuals on the subversion of African teachers and leaders into Red Chinese propagandists; pamphlets on the use of drugs to blind the mind and buy support; and a wealth of leads that would keep AXE's Moroccan Man, plus his newly arrived assistants, enthusiastically busy for weeks to come.

Nick and Liz stood hand in hand, like teenagers, hearing the planes roar in and out and gazing at each other. In a few minutes she would board her plane for Abimako, via Dakar. He would fly to Lisbon and then change for New York. She thought: I'll never see him again. And a wave of quiet despair washed over her.

"It's time," Nick said gently. "Don't forget me. There is a future and . . . who knows?"

She raised her hand and lightly brushed his cheek.

"I won't forget you," she whispered. "And please . . . remember, too." Then she turned quickly towards her plane.

Nick watched her go, his eyes full of her large-scale loveliness and his heart full of the nights they had spent together. Then he, too, walked toward his plane.

The touch of her fingers still tingled on his face.